AF416957

MAZE

HAROLD DEAN JAMES

Harold Dean James
Maze

All rights reserved
Copyright © 2023 byHarold Dean James

No part of this publication may be reproduced, distributed, or transmitted in any form or by any means, including photocopying, recording, or other electronic or mechanical methods, without the prior written permission of the publisher, except in the case of brief quotations embodied in critical reviews and certain other noncommercial uses permitted by copyright law.

Published by BooxAi
ISBN: 978-965-578-367-4

for
Kay Francis Byrd
1947-2018
and
Jesse Charles James
1948-2018

"There is love in me the likes of which you've never seen.
There is rage in me the likes of which should never escape.
If I am not satisfied in the one, I will indulge the other."

"It is true, we shall be monsters, cut off from all the world;
But on that account we shall be more attached to one another."

Mary Shelley's Frankenstein

CONTENTS

AUTHOR'S NOTE

Maze is a futuristic pleasure planet. Because of its blue sun which is hazardous to fairer skinned individuals, almost all the characters who live or visit Maze have dark skin with the exception of some of the characters inside of Lillum tanks. Lillum tanks are explained during the course of the novel.

1

———————

Through the lens of her magnoscanner, Candra was able to watch on every continent of the earth-like planet, obscenely tall buildings collapse onto each other, uniform and smooth pavements and streets break and separate into craters wide enough to require bridges to cross, and mile-wide tornadoes lifting and hurling everything out of their destructive path. This was all expected when an alien world was nearly colliding into the formally occupied planet that she watched from a safe distance. What was unexpected, was the lone dog trying to avoid the omnipresent harms.

"Oh Kos!" She exclaimed, "that poor dog. Arnie, isn't there anything we can do?"

Arnie, the ship's computer, popped up on a screen near Candra. He had a dark complexion and His upper body displayed a cleric's hat and white collar.

"All we can do is pray for it my dear. That's why we're this far away. Safety parameters, you know."

Candra ran her bronze fingers through her gold, curly locks.

"I can't watch anymore. Why would anyone leave a poor, defenseless puppy alone to face this nightmare?"

"You know you have a penchant for rescuing things in hopeless situations."

"Oh, I was wondering why I was with you. I'm going in."

Candra got up out of the com chair and started to remove her chainmail dress but was interrupted by Arnie's exclamation.

"Oh dear."

She turned back to the direction of one of the many screens showing the same catastrophic dance. The dog, after having hidden itself in a subway car, was lifted by a tornado from its home world onto the surface of the invading alien planet. The atmosphere was deteriorating there as well but at least there were no earthquakes or tornadoes. The dog limped out of the car sniffing around for something, anything, familiar but that seemed like an impossibility on its strange new home. It crawled back into the broken subway car.

"At least it's alive."

Arnie responded by piping in Staying Alive from Saturday Night Fever up all over the ship and Arnie now appeared in a white suit doing the familiar dance moves from the movie. Candra's spaceship was ten thousand miles above the too-close-to-each-other-planets, and resembled a large insect in space. It was green and yellow with silver wings and had an inscription on its side reading: O.R.E.S. 1600. The metal mandibles in front of the ship noiselessly and quickly ingested debris that had drifted away from the two planets, sifting through thousands of yards of remains, searching for anything of value. Inside the bug, a vast array of computers quietly hummed like monks chanting in a near coma while analyzing the debris. All the computers lit up on the rare occasion that it captured an item of interest or of value. The spacecraft estimated and recorded its monetary value, then stored the item. Afterwards, the computers all eventually returned to their dull lighting and low humming. Candra took off her dress which electromagnetically compensated for the non-gravitational effect inside the ship and pulled her slim but well-endowed body into her Lillum tank. As soon as she was inside, the computerized gas inside the tank generated gold medieval body armor on her with a helmet to match. Across from her, a half human, half reptilian green-skinned woman of larger proportions displayed her long tongue while licking her long sharp teeth. She was accompanied by two other similar creatures standing behind her who also licked their smiling chops while occasionally hissing. Fire poles lit up the night sky accompanied by a small ground fire separating the two warriors on a barren field of red dirt. The two women unsheathed their swords attached to their sides and the reptilian woman took several swipes at Candra who not only easily avoided her opponent's attempts but inflicted a few cuts on the scaly creature's arms and legs. Eventually, they locked blades with intense grins close enough to feel the heat from each other's breath. The reptilian woman displayed her array of long pointed teeth before speaking.

"I'm going to eat your pretty face Caaaandra."

"Well," Candra responded,

"that should at least improve your breath."

The reptilian woman dropped her sword, grabbed Candra's wrists and slammed her to the ground. Candra got up complaining.

"Damn! That *hurt!*"

Candra side-kicked the woman in the gut and jumped to her feet. Both had lost their swords. The larger woman charged. She wrapped her arms around Candra lifting her off the ground, trying to squeeze the life out of Candra and at the same time, attempting to eat Candra's face. In a surprising show of strength, Candra forced the woman's arms apart, grabbed her head and brought both of her knees into the woman's chin. The woman fell backwards to the ground. Candra quickly rolled her body into an upright position. Her opponent rose more slowly but charged again. This time Candra slid underneath and tripped her. Before she could get up, Candra landed several blows to the other woman's head with both of her fists. The reptilian woman viciously kicked Candra's right knee. She went down screaming. Her opponent grabbed a nearby sword, aimed it at Candra's head to deliver the final blow. Candra swerved out of the way. After avoiding a few more fatigued swings, Candra kicked the woman in the midsection. She followed with a series of blows to the head until Candra could barely distinguish her green facial features from her green blood as she lay motionless on the ground. Candra retrieved her sword and held it close to the reptilian's throat.

"Concede?" The reptilian grinned weakly.

"Next time human."

The reptilian's two friends helped her get up and walk away. Candra took off her helmet and smiled. Her mood was interrupted by the sight of Byryn limping towards her. He was tall like her, had a slightly darker complexion partially hidden by blood dripping from several places. She ran the short distance to him as he barely got the words out.

"Took your time…."

Byryn passed out and Candra lifted him off his feet.

"I should have killed that bitch!"

A chime sounded and Candra looked up.

"What is it?"

Arnie's ubiquitous voice from the night sky responded.

"Incoming star-mail, alpha one origin, priority one."

Candra gently placed Byryn on the ground and stroked his hair.

"Transmit."

A remarkably old, thin and sickly male face with metal gear and tubes attachments appeared in the night sky. He spoke with a partially mechanical voice.

"Hello Candy, long time no see or hear. I understand you're out in Yarr country near the Rylan cluster. Times must be rough. Anyway, I have an assignment for you, that is, if you're interested. Rumor has it that you've lost interest in our little club. That would be a pity for everyone but mostly you. I'll send the details of the assignment via com-link. The usual commish plus five points and please, don't forget the regular installment. Also, don't make me send another pi-one star mail to you. You know how expensive that is, and you know I'll bill you for it. Miss you Candy."

The man laughed but ended up coughing before his image faded from the night sky. Exhausted from the battle, Candra spoke in a half whisper.

"Kos damn son of a bitch bastard! Cease program."

Byryn and everything around her faded to black. An opening appeared and Candra, now garment-less, stepped out of a chamber and was propelled into the non-gravitational field of the ship. The ship mechanically fitted her into the bright silver, chain-mail dress which enabled her to walk normally inside of her ship. The side of the chamber Candra had stepped out of read 'Lillum gas simulation tank model A77ZXB58493-CNTP.' Candra walked over to the com and studied the compu-spectral graph.

"Oh come on Arnie, why are you bothering to store this crap?"

Arnie responded petulantly.

"As per your orders Madame, all common and uncommon artifacts, valuable, unknown potentially valuable".......

"All right, fine! Doesn't mean I can't bitch about it."

"Besides" Arnie spoke up, "you haven't scanned the collection in its entirety."

"Yeah, yeah, yeah." Candra replied, "what the hell is this?"

You could hear a suggestion of pride in Arnie's voice. "Byrinium Crystallo".

"Candra could not contain her excitement. "Byrinium crystals!"

"The same."

"Great! You found something of *real* value."

Arnie played back Candra's voice. "Yeah, yeah, yeah."

"Arnie, if you don't stop that I'll delete you!"

"Careful, I might voice-mail that threat to my lawyer."

"You go right ahead. By the time they find you, you'll be completely program wiped."

"This is being recorded, you know."

Candra gave Arnie the finger. "Record this!"

Candra looked over the spectral image of the crystals. "Arnie, what's the selling rate in B.R. credits for those crystals?"

"Low bred. I think you know Balkin Red credits are illegal in all three-hundred and forty-seven par-secs."

"Look" Candra fumed in a pretentious rage. "If I want a mother, I'll rent one. Answer the question!"

"For all you know, you may have one already and your rent is way overdue."

"Very funny."

"About time you acknowledge my clever wit. The crystals can be sold as Balkin red credits in the Catan Prine region and on planet Vree in the Dagron colony."

"Dagron colony, who the hell wants to go there?"

A translucent, crystalloid, three-dimensional face appeared above the com-screen.

"Not I, I assure you."

"Arnie, would you stop with the faces?"

"Stop with the voices, stop with the faces."

"Please, not now." Arnie's face popped out of view. "Get a location on the nearest Betan trade merchant."

"Anonymous inquiries?"

"As per usual."

"Time limit?"

"No, just let me know when the com link arrives."

"As per usual."

Candra pushed a few buttons on the com and had her garment removed. Without gravity, she pulled herself back into the Lillum tank. After she was in, a new face appeared above the com. Arnie tried a few different colors and hair styles before selecting one that simulated a blue Elvis Presley. He admired his new face and then smiled to reveal multi-colored teeth and finally, a long, pink tongue emerged that was shaped like a flute. Tiny appendages grew from the tongue and Arnie played a short selection from symphony number 40 by Mozart. He laughed at his accomplishment and his laughter and face slowly faded from view.

Millions of miles and moods away, a different face could be seen on large viewscreens. It was a dark-skinned human wearing heavy eye make-up and a laurel crown whose voice could be heard throughout an enormous disco arena. On stage, the singer was dressed like Julius Caesar with many knives sticking out of his back. The other band members, two guitarists, a drummer and a keyboard player, were wearing red leather in various styles. There were ten-foot stone statues of gladiators on either side of the band. Hundreds of people were dancing to the band's music or just watching them. All the people had dark skin. Across from the stage in a secluded area was a long, dimly lit bar. The bartender looked almost human but mostly looked bored. He was staring at a beautiful woman with big eyes accentuated by colorful makeup which included long eyelashes. The woman had long red hair with sparkles in it and wore a see-through cowgirl outfit which made it easy to notice her large breasts that didn't seem to be affected by gravity. A man who was terribly sunburnt with dark red splotches on his Caucasian skin, sat next to her. He was wearing the kind of suit cops wear, looked extremely ordinary but was trying to fit in. The woman looked at him, smiled, and he felt obligated to respond.

"Buy you a drink?"

"Do I look like I need one?"

The man looked at her half full glass. "No, not really."

She took a few sips and commented on his skin tone. "So, having fun in the sun?"

Robert's face became even redder. "Yeah, went out without my sun suit."

Not a very smart cowboy, are you?"

"Well, I didn't believe all the hype about this being a non-white people's planet."

"Made a believer outta you huh?"

"Sure as hell did."

While taking another few sips from her drink, the cowgirl's left breast began to move on its own. It slowly worked its way partially out of the bra, grew a small face and winked at the man. He stood up wide-eyed and she turned to him slightly raising her cowboy hat and smiled.

"What's wrong?"

The breast returned to normalcy. "Uh, your uh, your... nothing."

She stood up and he noticed her above average height. "Wanna dance cowboy?"

"Uh, Robert."

"What?"

"The name's Robert. What's yours?"

"Look cowboy, you wanna dance or not?"

"Sure, love to."

Robert and the cowgirl walked out to the dance floor just as the band finished a song. The crowd cheered and clapped enthusiastically but the lead singer gave a thumbs down to the audience and they become silent. One of the gladiators made of stone looked over the crowd, he then stiffly walked out to the middle of the floor. As he pointed his sword at several people, it emitted a beam of light that scanned their bodies. Their images were translated to the screens and the large crowd watched the selected people in the transmission get eaten by lions on the big screens. The crowd went wild. The music began again while the crowd yelled repeatedly,

"Hail Caesar! Hail Caesar!"

The cowgirl danced wildly and fluidly. Robert was stiff and awkward. He did not notice that she had left the floor until she was almost back at the bar.

"What's wrong, you didn't like the music?"

"No,... you can't dance."

"Oh, yeah,.... sorry."

"Can you fuck?"

In a much smaller and darker room, a woman was yelling,

"That's it cowboy! Ride me! Ride me like a rough rider! Hang on! That's it! Oh yeah! Oh yeah!"

It was the cowgirl yelling, and Robert was on top of her with nothing on but her see-through cowboy hat and a scarf. A pained expression inhabited Robert's face as he tried his best to satisfy the woman he met at the disco arena. She placed her hands on his bare buttocks and her hands melded together. Robert started to moan with ecstasy, but his moans soon become screams as his body slowly dissolved into the cowgirl who now resembled a giant luminous slug with four translucent antennae sticking out the sides of her larger, rich, dark chocolate human head. Tentacles grew from the side of her slug-like form and removed her hat from him while immensely enjoying Robert dissolving into her as if it were the most incredible sex she ever had. Her irises were now bright green as she finished consuming him. The physimager changed back into her human form, dressed herself and grew a few more sparkles into her face and hair before leaving Robert's room with a smirk on her face.

"You can't fuck either."

CHAPTER 2

Leaning her pole against the cave wall, Candra used the gloved back of her left hand, moist from humidity, to wipe sweat from her brow. She paused in the thick atmosphere to watch large green and black lizards crawling between narrow paths of molten lava that emitted sulfurous smoke and red glowing light. Her tan khaki shorts and shirt were soaked with sweat. Candra took a length of rope from her waist, cut it and tied her machete to the pole to use it as a weapon. As she came upon a wide path of lava, she sized it up, took a dozen steps back and used the pole to vault over the hot flow. Unfortunately, there were five hungry lizards waiting for her. She crushed one landing and killed two with her improvised spear. One lizard bit onto the spear but she managed to push it into the lava until only its head remained. The surviving lizard decided to find a less difficult meal and crawled away. Candra saw what she came for in this hazardous cave, a tall black tree with few branches and no leaves.

On the branches, were a few pieces of bright blue fruit. Climbing up on a mound, she untied the machete and tied the remaining rope to the end of the pole and hurled it high up into the tree. The branches of the tree caught the pole while a mouth formed and the tree started to consume the pole. When the slack in the rope was diminished, Candra held onto it and swung towards the tree with the machete between her teeth. The branches tried to capture her but she used the machete to discourage them. She climbed to a point where she could pick the blue fruit, did so, and jumped away from the tree. The tree vibrated violently, grew spears and used its branches to hurl them at her. Candra managed to avoid the spears, quickly hiding behind a boulder.

She studied the flow of lava nearby, too wide to jump across and gathered several spears to throw them into the burning river. When the black tree's spear throwing slowed, Candra ran to the lava river and used the upper part of the spears to hoist her way across the molten lava. Just as she landed on solid ground, a spear hit her in the back. She fell forward onto the hard, red ground and could hear Arnie's familiar giggle.

"Real fucking funny Arnie."

Candra took the small bright blue fruit, raised it to her dry lips and squeezed out a few drops. She then decided to take a nap while the fruits juice worked its magic.

Half an hour later, Candra saw the spear that had been imbedded in her back, lying next to her. She felt no pain and could not tell where the former injury was. She looked with pleasure at the healing fruit before placing it in her pocket. When she looked up, she saw one more lizard smiling who foolishly thought she might be its next meal. Candra took up her machete. After another thirty minutes, Candra was back near the fire poles. This time, the full moon added to the existing light. The last lizard Candra had encountered was still smiling but roasting on a spit. She administered a few drops of the blue fruit into Byryn's mouth and his breathing slowed and became normal. His wounds began to heal and he was finally able to utter words.

"You saved me again."

"That's my job."

"Some job you have."

Candra ripped a piece of meat off the spit. "Try and eat something."

Byryn started slowly but as more healing occurred, began eating like the food deprived person he was.

"Easy tiger."

Saliva was dripping down his mouth as he spoke. "This is really good. Where'd you get it?"

"You don't want to know."

Byryn slowed his eating pace. "Let me guess, some place where you almost get killed again."

Candra watched Byryn relax and approached him with water and a smile. "You're worth it."

"Yeah, well thank you but I don't want to do this anymore."

"What! What are you talking about?"

"Ahh come on Candra. Our whole existence is you rescuing me! What kind of a life is that? You do the fighting. I do the running and hiding."

Candra gently placed her left hand on Byryn's slightly bearded face. "That's all we do?"

Byryn blushed.

"Well, no. But come to think of it, why is it that the only time we have any peace and quiet is when we're making love?"

Candra smiled broadly. "I don't know, perhaps we're not making love enough?"

The thought had not occurred to Byryn and he stopped eating. "Really?"

"I think it's worth investigating." Candra took off her top. Byryn stood up and started taking off his clothes while admiring the view standing in front of him. "You might be right."

CHAPTER 3

Captain Helance Mozilli looked at the picture of Robert Callins on the com screen in his dimly lit office. He slid his wide fingers across the screen to get a few different views of the only white man on Maze, now presumed deceased. Mozilli's face looked like a combination of unremarkable slits that seemed to express that he was indefinitely in pain. He looked away from the screen and up at the two detectives standing across from him. Observing them seemed to increase his discomfort. Nevertheless, he turned the screen towards them.

"Either one of you see this guy before?"

The men looked at a picture of the severely sunburnt man after he was released from a first aid clinic. Felker spoke up.

"Isn't that the white guy who stepped outside without a sunsuit?"

Mozilli shook his head. "By god Felker, you are a detective aren't you?"

Felker, whose nose and lips were too big and always looked like he was never really awake always spoke for the two of them.

"He's not on the missing tourist list, is he?"

Mozilli sighed. "Yep, and he's G.B.I."

"G.B.I.?"

Wex blurted out. Mozilli looked at him with annoyance because when he rarely did say something, it was as if he were underwater. It was bad enough that he looked like a fish, enormous eyes, long narrow head and ears that seemed to be slightly twitching all the time. But if fish could talk Mozilli thought, they would sound like Wex.

"Now don't get your feathers all ruffled fellas, special agent Callins was here like everyone else, having a little fun, just.... as a tourist."

Felker and Wex looked relieved that the GBI agent was not here to scrutinize their work. The police department was better known as the "lost and found department" here on Maze and Mozilli knew that. He also knew his detectives were too incompetent to do any real police work. Fortunately, crime on the pleasure planet had been reduced to a few misplaced valuables that were usually found and not so much by the detectives. To counter missing persons, everyone on Maze wore a wrist-com. The wrist-com was a screen on the skin between two almost imperceptible wires from the wrist and half-way to the elbow. Callins wrist-com had disappeared along with Callins. "Maybe he's AWOL." Felker suggested.

"Well, that's a possibility Felker, albeit an unlikely one since he told them this is where he was going. Nevertheless, the Galactic Bureau of Investigation has lost a man and it is our job to find him."

Mozilli could see the stress on his detectives faces at the prospect of doing some actual work. He almost smiled at the thought of it.

"That is," he continued, "we at least have to do a preliminary report. As you know, the GBI takes care of its own and this is no exception.

They'll be sending an agent who will make himself known to us. When he arrives...."

This time Mozilli could not help but smile broadly. "...you two will have the honor and privilege of working with him."

Mozilli could see the panic on Felker's face, and Wex looked like he was gasping for air.

"Now, I know you ladies are all flustered and everything but please,... have a little dignity. Besides, I haven't told you the good part."

The detectives were too afraid to ask what the 'good part' might be so Mozilli stood up, leaned towards them and spoke in a hushed tone.

"When the gid gets here, the three of you will go pay a visit to Ozoz."

Wex's eyes got impossibly wider and his ears started twitching furiously. Felker had a hard time getting the words out.

"Is this some kind of joke Captain? Cause if it is, I'm not amused." Mozilli raised one barely haired eyebrow.

"Have you ever been amused in *life* Felker?" Anyway, I've made special arrangements for you princesses. And, Ozoz has personally guaranteed your safety." Mozilli grimaced. "Unfortunately, the both of you may actually live through this ordeal."

Felker walked towards the door but turned back.

"YOU CAN'T BE SERIOUS! Only *one* person has gone to see Ozoz has come back alive and wouldn't talk about it. You know that! He, or whatever that thing is, doesn't answer to anybody! Special arrangements my ass! I'm not going on a suicide mission and neither is Wex. You can have our badges if you want em. For Kos sake, why don't you set up some kind of com-link with 'em or something?"

Mozilli sat back down and took his time answering.

"As unlikely as it may seem, a com-link has been set up with Ozoz through the chairman's office. That was a long time ago Felker. And, the ad hoc arrangements we made was that the two of you and the GBI agent will have a private audience with Ozoz. Furthermore, I don't give a dead Turruglian's ass if you like the arrangement or not. Neither the Chairman's office nor I like the fact that now there are five tourists and three residents missing, far exceeding the norm and no apparent leads from either one of you. Does that fairly assess the situation lieutenant?"

Felker swallowed hard and looked downwards. "Yes sir."

Mozilli continued. "Well, now that the MazeCor committee has..."

"MazeCor?" Wex blurted out.

Mozilli gave him an exasperated look. "That's right Wex, the almighty MazeCor financial committee has got the GBI involved because they have no confidence in our abilities. You ladies will get to see up close how a real cop works."

There was a moment of silence in the room as all three cops were contemplating the foreseeable changes in their future.

Finally, Wex spoke up. "Captain, what if Ozoz himself is causing these disappearances?"

"Yeah." Felker added.

Mozilli leaned back in his chair. "Well, then you will have finally done what you're getting paid to do, won't you?"

"Yeah" Felker continued, "and what if we don't come back?"

The two detectives looked at Mozilli like there would be some sort of reprieve, a kind of retraction but it was clear there would be no such thing coming.

"There's always that chance isn't there? That's the nature of police work isn't it? Now get the hell out of my office. You're giving me a fucking headache."

Mozilli watched the detectives slowly shuffle out of his office. He opened his desk drawer and pulled out a Tylenol lolly-pop. Unwrapping the candy meticulously, he looked at his closed door, placed the lolly in his mouth and his smile gradually made its way back.

CHAPTER 4

Sixteen-thousand miles away from a circular cluster of crystal meteorites, a shuttle the size and length of two football fields silently glided by. Eighty percent of the ship's cargo wereLillum tanks. Inside the bow of the ship, hundreds of lit panels displayed the ship's trajectory, maintenance and life support. The near endless rows of Lillum tanks were like metallic cocoons with wires and tubes attached to them. Inside one of the larger tanks, a family of four was being led by a small pixie. All of them had over-sized dragonfly wings and the pixie was leading them in flight above a simulated landscape of the planet Maze under its blazing blue sun. Currently below them was a labyrinth made from tall garden hedges and beyond that, the pixie pointed to an enormous field where a few brontosauruses were grazing.

"Maze has the largest natural garden labyrinth in the known universe. Guests spend anywhere from a few days to a few months lost in the maze with plenty of adventures at every turn. Up ahead is Jurassic Village, home of the ichthyosaurs, plesiosaurs, stegosaurus and tyrannosaurus rex. There is a rex heading our way now.

"Watch out! Whew, that was close."

The boy in the family, Brad, rolled his eyes. "Oh Kos!"

Bradley's father shook his head. "Freeze program."

The pixie, dinosaurs and the wings that enabled the family to fly, froze in place as the father turned to his son.

"I'm sorry if you're bored Bradly but we **ALL** agreed to come here for vacation. Didn't we?"

"Dad,.. I got the same dumb programs at home."

"Oh come on. Nobody's got this kind of sophisticated computer simulation back...."

"They got **ALL** this at game world!"

"Game World?"

Brad's Mother interrupted. "Bradley, give it a chance honey. Your sister is. Look how happy she is."

Bradley knew what to expect but he looked anyway. His younger sister Lillie was wide eyed and wore the same simple smile she always did. Bradley often thought she was mildly retarded but knew what kind of madness to expect from his parents if he decided to entertain that notion with them. Instead, he said what was expected of him.

"Well, as long as Lillie's happy."

Bradley's Father could hear the sarcasm in Brad's voice but decided to continue with the tour.

"I'm sure we'll come across more than a few things that are not in 'Game World.' Resume program."

Bradley's Mother came closer to him.

"Bradley, the programs here are a lot more real than the ones in Game World. You know that don't you?"

Bradley focused on the pixie who was now taking them towards ski lifts.

"I don't like real. Real is dangerous."

Bradley's Mother smiled in response to Bradley's comment, but she was worried more than usual about her impossible-to-please son.

In a Lillum tank not too far from the family, an elderly woman sat in a comfortable bed looking over several women of various sizes, ages and uniqueness attributed to their planet of origin. A computerized voice made an announcement.

"This completes your selection. As per your instructions, the escorts you have selected will meet you individually at specified locations over the course of your stay on Maze. If for any reason you or your guests are not satisfied at any time with any of the selected escorts, do not hesitate to contact us for an immediate replacement."

The woman raised her wrist-com to her lips.

"Mel,... Mel, are you ready?"

A panel slid open and the woman's bed joined an elderly man's bed, Mel, lying next to a young and beautiful green woman in a pink negligée. Mel kissed the green woman on the forehead.

"Goodbye Natalie." Natalie smiled and disappeared.

"You sure you don't want to keep her?"

Mel looked over the women Sylvia had selected for him.

"I don't think so Sylvia. I think you outdid yourself this time."

"Yes, I think I did. And what, pray to tell, did you get for me?"

Mel sat up in the bed.

"Just you wait and see my dear. Computer, next program." Several men from short to very tall in various darker skin hues and abnormal hair growths appeared.

Sylvia smiled broadly.

"Ohhh, nice job. I especially like the one with the tail." Mel smiled. "I thought you might."

They both grinned while looking over the various male and female selections. Inside of a Lillum tank further down the extensive row, there was the dim signal of a flashlight at the end of a corridor in a poorly lit warehouse. Returning the signal at the other end of the corridor, were men dressed in long coats who looked like they came out of a gangster movie from the 1920s on earth. They were approaching the other group of gangsters. One of the men, Big Ed, watched them as they approached. He had a long face and spoke as if there was an unfortunate taste in his mouth.

"They're here Sallie."

Sallie was seated in a comfortable office chair. He was a thick man who seemed to be finishing the last few chews of a meal, when in fact, he was not. He smiled in a condescending way, drummed with his fingers and addressed the large man in front of the group wearing a long, blue, cashmere coat.

"You're late Georgie boy. Lucky I don't charge you interest." Ugly George ignored Sallie.

"Where's the girl?" Sallie looked over Ugly George with disgust and turned his head towards Big Ed. Big Ed grabbed a young, pretty, dark-skinned female with blonde hair and forced her into the light. Her hands were tied and her mouth taped. Ugly George looked over the young lady and smiled.

"Bring her closer." Sallie held up one hand. "She's close enough."

There was a moment of silence as the two bosses stared at each other and nobody moved. Finally, Ugly George laughed and motioned to one of his goons and a suitcase was placed near Sallie. Sallie opened the suitcase and looked over the stacks of bills. "OK" he said with a fake smile. Big Ed escorted the unwilling lady to Ugly George who kissed her with the tape over her mouth. She struggled and he laughed again. As Ugly George and his men started to leave, Sallie muttered, "Sick fuck."

The two groups of gangsters abruptly stopped their departure at the sound of someone sweeping. When the sweeper came into view, it was a short, skinny, dorky looking young man wearing glasses and pushing a broom. He looked at the two groups of gangsters but did not seem to be concerned. "Oh, uh, excuse me."

The gangsters watched the sweeper for a moment before Big Ed spoke.

"Hey, what the hell you doing?"

The sweeper continued his chore. "Uh.... cleaning?"

After a moment, Ugly George laughed, and all the gangsters joined in. The dorky sweeper got caught in the laughter as well but Ugly George was only feigning the humor. "Waste em."

The men from both groups pulled semi-automatic machine guns from underneath their long coats and unloaded their clips. When they were done, they attached new clips to their guns and looked at where the sweeper used to be. A broken part of the broomstick rolled away from a pile of bloody rags. The men continued their departure until they heard the sweeper's voice.

"That wasn't very nice."

Before they could start shooting again, the sweeper became a blur and upon returning to his spot, all but the two bosses were lying on the floor. The sweeper smiled broadly before speaking.

"I would show you that again, but your boys are all unconscious." Ugly George released his grip on the girl. He and Sallie drew large handguns and fired at the sweeper. The sweeper easily dodged all the bullets and spoke behind them.

"You know what they say fella's, once bitten twice shy." He slammed their heads together and the two bosses fell to the floor. He walked over to the young lady and untied her hands. She gently pulled the tape off her mouth, kissed him and then slapped him hard.

"About time!"

The sweeper rubbed the finger marks on his face. "Ow! That's gratitude! Let's get out of here before they wake up."

The sweeper's cleaning outfit turned into a superhero costume. He placed his arm around the young lady's waist and the two of them flew off together. On a bright, sunny day created by the Lillum tank next to the Sweeper's, an athletic man in his early thirties, served a tennis ball to an attractive woman in her mid-forties. After a furious rally, the man hit the ball beyond the service line and the match ended. They both sat on the bench mid-court with towels draped over their head and shoulders. Still breathing heavily, the man, Jacques, took the towel off his head and spoke. "I don't know Sam, I think I oughta stop letting you win."

Samantha slid the towel off her head and laughed. "Well, better luck next time. Oh Kos! I need a swim and a snooze. I'll see you on the return flight, okay Jacques?" Jacques peered intensely into Samantha's eyes, smiled, and started to disappear.

"Wait, Jacques,... give me a goodbye kiss."

Jacques' smile became broader as he fully appeared again and he and Sam locked lips and arms. He disappeared again while Sam was still trying to hold him.

"It never lasts long enough."

The sky turned orange while the tennis court was transformed into a cliff overlooking a sparkling crystal-blue lake with paisley flowers floating on the surface. Sam took off her tennis whites and dived off the edge of the cliff. She swam to a shore of sparkling white sand and approached a tent on the small beach area. Inside the tent, Sam climbed into a large circular bed. After pulling the comforter over herself, Sam closed her eyes and moments later re-opened them.

"Jacques, I think I'm gonna need help falling asleep." The comforter swelled into Jacques' form lying next to her.

"Do you need a massage?" He asked, whispering.

Sam turned to him. "Well, sort of." Jacques' amazing smile came back. "OK, I'll start with the feet." Sam leaned upwards. "You're kidding?"

"Yes" he said and started kissing her neck. Samantha giggled like a little schoolgirl.

At the end of the long rows of Lillum tanks, a man sat alone with a dark beer in his faintly-lit cubicle. He looked through the simulated porthole, towards the planet being formed by the cluster of crystal meteorites and studied the inscription at the bottom of the rounded sill. It read "Robert Lillum." This man, Brian Bicks, with the exception of his larger forehead, had a remarkable resemblance to Candra's Byryn. He smiled, thinking of how after the young inventor, Robert Lillum, invented a gas that could be programmed to create any world one desired inside of a tank, never left his own personal tank until they removed his dead body. After that, all the

Lillum tanks were equipped with interior and exterior life support monitors. Brian examined the interior monitors. They indicated that he was in good health and that the ship was operating within its normal parameters. He stared at the monitor until it started resembling his screen at GBI headquarters. He remembered Fulmore's big, bald head fill the screen with his dependable, insincere smile.

"New job for you Bicky boy."

Bick's hated the way Fulmore called him 'Bicky boy' but countered with what he knew Fulmore also hated being called.

"What's that, More Full?"

The feigned smile on the monitor turned into a frown.

"You've got an assignment on Maze, the pleasure planet."

Bicks took a sip. "But I take it there's no pleasure involved."

"Is there ever? One of our agents disappeared there and you get to find out why."

"Sounds like a good place to disappear."

"We thought so too but the same thing has happened to more than a few tourists, you'll have to act quickly and discreetly. MazeCor wants to keep this under the radar."

Bicks smiled wryly while looking over his stat-com. "Yeah, Kos forbid they should lose any money over this. Maze is one hundred and twenty-four par-secs away. Why am I being sent?

"Perhaps you haven't heard. Maze likes people with a darker complexion, not pale fella's like me."

"Oh, right," Bicks added. "It's the blue sun."

"Yeah" Fulmore continued, "so you're the lucky duck being plucked Bicky boy. You'll be working with the local enforcement and report to a Captain Mozilli. They'll want to equip you with a local wrist-com but you won't need it."

"Always under surveillance. Who's the agent?"

"Robert Callins."

"Callins? Isn't he a white fella?"

"He was." Fulmore smiled and ended the conversation. "Bye bye Bicky boy." His face faded on the monitor and Bicks spoke to the on-board computer named after the inventor's daughter.

"Roberta, bedding, soft with a large pillow." The desk Bicks was sitting at became a bed. He finished his beer, lay back, and once again stared at the forming crystal planet.

CHAPTER 5

On an endless beach with black sand underneath the blue sun of Maze, a dark-skinned blonde-haired couple rode bronze horses with blonde manes. As they headed towards the small castle where they had a limited time share, Shakree, the male, pointed at something near the water. His partner, Sheela yelled over the galloping.

"What is it?"

"I don't know."

Shakree dismounted and started to walk towards the strange object partially buried in the sand and Sheela did the same. When he got close enough he laughed. "I think it's a mermaid."

"Is it alive?"

"You oughta know, you planted it."

"I did not! It looks like something you would do."

"Ha, if I did this, it would definitely be alive."

"A dead mermaid in Fantasy World. That's so weird. If neither one of us planted this, we should leave it alone. They warned us about unexpected plants."

"Aw come on Sheela, for all we know, your parents might have planted this. Help me throw it back into the water, maybe she'll come back to life."

"Maybe she'll come back to life? You jerk! You did plant this, didn't you?"

"No, really, I didn't. You gonna help me or what?"

"It looks heavy."

"No worries." Shakree turned the mermaid body over onto her back and admired the large breasts. "I'll take the heavy end."

"Jerk."

The face of the mermaid was the same as the cowgirl at the disco-arena. Along the stretch of the beach, the two bronze horses with the blonde manes ran off together. Faint screams were heard from a distance as the horses galloped away from the couple. In the darkness of an enormous office, a man's eyes gave off a dim glow. His visually enhanced eyes were looking at stat-graph visuals of various people who were recently reported missing. A buzz distracted him from the screen.

"Who is it?"

"Kelde."

Kelde was a very thin man with a bad complexion. He could not help but see the glowing eyes and walked towards them through the large dark office and comparable desk. He stood there while the man continued to look over his files. Kelde finally spoke up.

"May we have some light?"

"Why?"

Kelde always had a smile on his face for no apparent reason. "I'd like to see your handsome face."

"I'll send you a picture. What have you got for me?"

"Nothing good I'm afraid."

"Let me guess, another disappearance."

"Two, actually."

"Kos. Take a seat Kelde."

Kelde sat in front of the desk and dropped a pic-disk of Shakree and Sheela Dubois.

The man's wide hands picked up the disk and studied the picture of the couple.

Shakree and Sheela carried the mermaid towards the beach. Sheela stopped for a moment.

"Kos, next time you plant something, don't make it so heavy."

"Sheela, I really didn't plant this. You wanna leave it here?"

"Ha, we're almost at the water, what's the point? It's okay, now I'm into this *mermaid rescue mission*. We throw it into the water and then maybe it comes back to life. Right?"

"Hell if I know. But what's the harm?"

"Oh, there's gonna be plenty of harm if you don't stop staring at her tits!"

Shakree laughed out loud and the creature opened her eyes and smiled. Back in his office, the man behind the large desk was staring at the picture of Sheela and Shakree. Kelde spoke up again. "The good news is, we found out they were gone almost immediately. They were a young couple, both doctors on an expensive honeymoon their parents paid for, and there were status alarms installed everywhere they went. Without their knowledge of course."

"Of course. That's the good news? Any other evidence?"

"Apparently they were killed by some kind of sea creature."

"Sea creature?"

"Yes, with a large tail fin and arms on the torso. The creature seemed to have consumed them."

"As well as their wrist-coms."

"Yes."

"Different perp, same outcome. What's the bad news?"

"The bad news is that we will be having a shareholder's meeting sooner rather than later."

The big man leaned back into his chair and turned the lights up marginally. "To cover their asses so they won't lose any money."

Kelde's smile got broader. "And ours."

"Make sure you make arrangements for that meeting before they do."

"Already done."

There was a strong breeze on the beach picking up the spray of clear blue water splashing onto the rocks near where Shakree and Sheela were swinging the mermaid.

"On three!" Shakree yelled above the waves. Before they could release the mermaid, two cords grew out of the ends of her large tail fin and wrapped around Sheela's waist. She screamed and Shaklee dropped the creature's torso and ran to her. As he tried to separate Sheela from the cords, they grew thicker and wrapped around Shaklee as well imprisoning them both. The mermaid grew into its larger, monstrous slug-like form that had consumed Robert Callins. Tentacles grew out of it and lifted both Shakree and Sheela off the ground and the monster grinned at the sound of their screams.

He turned off his stat-com and placed the pic-disk of Shakree and Sheela on top of his large, artificial wood desk. Sighing deeply before re-engaging Kelde he asked, "What about Ozoz?"

Kelde regained his smile.

"The meeting is all arranged. Wex and Felker will both have open channels on their wrist-coms.

"Think it will work this time?"

"No, we can't even re-establish our com-link with Ozoz."

"Are you the only one aware of that?"

"Yes."

"Good. What about bugging the GBI agent?"

"Too risky, he'll have his own bugs and scanners which will undoubtedly detect ours."

"You still think Ozoz has nothing to do with these disappearances?"

Kelde's smile grew impossibly wider. "Yes, if he did, you would have been the first to go."

Sheela and Shakree were suspended in the air. Sheela cried and Shakree yelled at the slug-like creature that had now grown to its full twelve-foot length with an over-sized human head. The creature was grinning wildly, and its four antennae on the side of its head were moving about erratically. It plunged the couple head-first into its green, fluorescent body and Shakree and his new bride slowly dissolved, as did their screams. The creature moaned loudly with ecstatic pleasure.

The large shadowy figure of a man picked up the pic-disk again and looked at the two bronze horses running on the beach. Kelde interpreted. "We found pic-scans of the horses. Apparently synthesized to resemble the owners."

He repeated Kelde's word slowly. "A p p a r e n t l y. No cross references to the others missing and no clues as to the identity of the perp?"

Kelde looked at his boss with more sincerity than usual. "Your assumption is correct. There was one sandal nearby, an obvious struggle between the missing couple and the creature and finally, footprints walking away, female we think. That's all I have." The large man did not look satisfied. "Send Mozilli over early tomorrow. I'll want to chew on his backside a while before special agent Bicks gets here."

Kelde walked towards the door in the poorly lit room but was stopped by the sound of his boss' voice. "Kelde."

"Yes, sir?"

"You really think I have a handsome face?"

The lights came up full this time to reveal that the man behind the desk slightly resembled a cat. Kelde just smiled and walked out the door. The lights faded again and when the door was closed, bold letters floating in glass could be read above the center of the door. "Phillimus Mekkel, chairman, MazeCor."

A field of tall grass glistened under the luminescence of an unusually large and full white moon. On closer inspection, the field revealed that some of the grass had been pushed aside or pulled out. The muffled sound of moaning and struggling was heard near the disturbed grass and getting nearer to the noises, the grass had been flattened out by two naked bodies now lying down and breathing heavily. The bodies belonged to Byryn and Candra. She got up and began to dress. Byryn started to get up but sank back down onto the earth.

"What's wrong?"

Byryn had difficulty responding. "I feel dizzy."

Candra laughed loudly and Byryn joined in. "Candra?"

"Yes?"

"Will you marry me?"

All traces of humor left Candra's face. "What?"

"Will you...."

"I heard you the first time. No."

"No? Why not?"

"I can't believe this. Why do you want to get married? How do you even know about marriage?"

"I'm not sure."

"Arnie!"

A face looking like an angel appeared in the moon and spoke. "Yes, my love."

"You told him about *marriage*?"

"You insisted that some of the programming remain mysterious."

Byryn looked up. "Who are you talking to?"

"Nobody!" Candra glared at Byryn but then approached him with a smile and sat next to him.

"Okay, why do you want to marry me?"

Byryn gave Candra a puzzled look. "Because I love you. Isn't that obvious? Don't...don't you love me?"

"Yes Byryn, of course I love you but,...."

"But what?"

"Well, Kos! You are *programmed* to love me."

"Yes, I am. I am programmed to be the best mate you will ever have. The perfect lover, the perfect husband and the perfect father to your children."

"Whoa,... what?"

"Don't you want to have children?"

Candra could not hide the surprise on her face. She tried to say something, but words failed her. Finally, she looked at Byryn and said "Hold that thought. I gotta go talk to nobody again."

She walked away perplexed and looked up at Arnie's face in the moon while shaking her head.

"What am I supposed to say to him Arnie?"

"Just go for it child. It'll be a hoot."

"A hoot?"

"Mmm hmm. And if it doesn't work out, ahh, you can program wipe the whole thing."

"Program wipe a baby?"

"Or keep it as an alternative program."

"You got this all figured out, don't you?'"

"That's my job."

In the background Byryn was jumped from behind, gagged and carried off on a horse by three gun-slinging cowgirls with beards.

"What about the uh,…pregnancy?"

Several moons with baby faces appeared around Arnie. All of them were giggling.

"How many babies we talking about shuggah?"

"One is more than enough Arnie." The baby moons popped out of view and Arnie took on a baby face. "Will it look like me?"

"Kos! I hope not. You don't even know what you look like."

Arnie's face starts crying like a baby.

"Oh, knock it off. What I mean is, can we cut the gestation period down?"

"In a hurry to get the little bugger out? Humph, you can have it today if you want. But,..you must follow the rules of the game."

"*Your* rules."

"I am the program master."

"The disaster master."

"Be careful, you could give birth to a camel."

"That's not funny Arnie."

"It could be." A half human, half camel baby appeared. Arnie giggled.

"Arnie!"

"You have a com-link coming in."

"What is it?"

"It's that job old and sickly was telling you about."

"Not interested."

"This job could pull us out of debt Candra. And it doesn't sound bad at all. But it will put us back into the homicide business. There is a killer loose on Maze, the pleasure planet. The local authorities are completely baffled and word is, GBI is getting involved."

"GBI?"

"It appears as though one of their own is a victim. Apparently they just disappear with the exception of a few articles of clothing or nothing at all. There is a bonus plus commission that keeps going up per week for anyone who can stop or ID the killer."

"A bonus plus commish, sounds terribly tempting. What's the catch?"

"Your employer."

"Who is it Satan?"

"Some people think so. Anyway, it goes by the name of Ozoz. An indigenous, non-physical, sub-surface dweller. The entity is believed to be...."

Candra looked in the direction of Byryn. "Where's Byryn?"

"Captured by the Pagwan."

"Damn! Well at least they won't torture him." Candra started walking towards where Byryn was last seen.

"Not in the conventional sense."

Candra stopped. "What does that mean?"

"I thought you liked surprises."

"Arnie!"

"The females control the town. They will drug him and force him to make love to most of the women…"

"What?"

"…..and you will have to negotiate to reclaim possession of him."

"And there are a few surprises you're not telling me about."

"Of course. What's life without a few surprises?"

"Or way more than a few. What else do you have on Ozoz?"

"The entity is believed to be as old as the planet itself. In fact, it seems like it is a permanent part of the planet."

"Well, at least he won't be hard to find."

"I don't know if I'd call it a he."

"Whatever. Anything else?"

"It is capable of affecting gravity to a certain extent and is also a suspect in the case."

"This is the thing I'm supposed to report to?"

"Yes indeedy."

The terrain had become more wooded as Candra walked through. She noticed broken twigs and horse shoe prints and followed the trail. "So how am I supposed to find this,... Ozoz?"

"My information conveys that at the right time, Ozoz will find you."

"Oh great! A non-human suspect wants to hire me."

Arnie's head popped into view again. This time, he was wearing a Sherlock Holmes type hat and monocle and spoke with a British accent. "Us Watson, *we're* being hired. I am the brainpower behind his joint venture."

"Did you say the brain fart part of this joint venture? Bonus plus commission huh?"

"Are you addressing me?"

"Yes, fool."

"I don't answer to that."

"Remember what I said earlier about being program wiped."

"Dear lord! It appears you are actually threatening me. I believe I shall consider consulting legal counsel about this matter."

"Consider illegal extinction."

"OH!" Arnie exclaimed as he popped out of view. Candra continued through the wooded area in pursuit of her lover Byryn and noticed that Arnie had suddenly programmed in more than a few prickly vines in her path. Candra was not sure but she swore she could hear a subtle giggle coming from where she last saw Arnie.

CHAPTER 6

There was only one spaceport on Maze, but it was large enough to accommodate the constant flow of space shuttles leaving and departing. The two runways were three-hundred feet above the space terminal and there were four over-sized elevators taking travelers to and from the landing sites. Since everyone on Maze stayed at hotels, a carryall with the hotel insignia would automatically take visitors and their luggage to their assigned hotel. Detectives Felker and Wex sat patiently in a marked vehicle waiting to escort special agent Brian Bicks to what they considered an unpleasant appointment. Wex watched the automated people-carts and luggage-carts whiz by while Felker watched his favorite soap opera on his wrist-com. Wex looked at his wrist-com and wiped the sweat from his forehead. He looked agitated and his whiskers stood out more than usual. "Felk?"

Felker had no intention of looking away from his wrist-com. "Hmmm?"

"What if they were planning on us disappearing?"

"What?"

"Think about it. We go see Ozoz. He zaps us or whatever the hell he does and we're history. We've solved the case but we're history!"

Felker regretfully put this soap on pause. "Wex, cut the crap. You know Ozoz hasn't done anything to anybody since they first discovered him."

Felker's calm tone did not appease Wex. "That sounds like every criminal, innocent until they're caught in the act!"

Felker lost his patience. "Look, will you quit bugging out! First of all, do you actually think GBI is gonna send another gid down here just so he can get himself whacked?" "Not likely. Secondly, what makes you think dealing with Ozoz will be any worse than dealing with those freaking Pelkin Sectoids?"

"Oh yeah, YEAH! You're right! It's one Kos damn shit job after another. That's what we're here for. Shit and then,...... MORE SHIT! (he yells into his wrist com) COME ON MOZILLI! PILE ANOTHER SHIT JOB ON US! AND WHEN YOU'RE FINISHED DUMPING THIS LOAD, WHY DON'T YOU SIT YOUR FAT ASS ON IT? CAUSE WE CAN TAKE THAT SHIT TOO!!"

Felker returned to his soap. "That's gonna cost ya."

"I don't care if he can hear us. I hope he can smell my farts too!"

Felker laughed. "He's not the only one listening."

"What, who else?"

"Oh the MazeCor chair, probably."

Felker covered his wrist-com with his free hand. "FUCK!!"

"Yeah you more than likely are man. Mozilli at worst will demote you but those feckless bastards on the chair will ship your ass outta here pronto." The detective's wrist-coms beeped. "The gids here. Listen, don't sweat it. You'll make up for it. Felker talked to his wrist-com. "Felker to HQ." Mozilli's face appeared on their wrist-coms.

"What is it?"

"Captain, the gids shuttle just landed."

"Right, call me when you reach the Ozoz location. Wex?"

Wex could see Mozilli's wide smile on his wrist-com. "Yes, captain?"

"You're a real Bat Masterson, you know that?"

"Yes sir."

Brian Bicks was in the rear of the large elevator descending from the shuttle strip. He noticed that everyone had been given wrist-coms before leaving the shuttle. The shuttle automatically inserted a small implant on everyone's left wrist which visually expanded to a four inch, skin thin, color screen that was active around the clock. Brian's GBI wrist-com incorporated the required Maze device. Other passengers in the lift included Samantha, the family of four and the dork with his girlfriend. The passengers did not have far to walk to their transports as they were all lined up in various colors with the passengers names on them in LED screens. The transports automatically connected to everyone's wrist-coms and took them to their hotels where their luggage awaited in their rooms. Brian's transport took him to the two detectives who looked like they were bored out of their skulls until he got close enough for them to recognize him. Just as he just stepped out of his ride and attempted to greet Felker and Wex, a piece of luggage slammed into him almost knocking him over. He looked at the black metal case and the owner who was right behind it asking him "Are you alright?" Brian looked at the attractive middle-aged woman dressed in black to match her luggage and replied. "I'm fine. I thought luggage was supposed to transport directly to your hotel?"

Samantha smiled wryly. "It is but I directed it to run into you."

"Why would you do that?"

"So I could nurse you back to health."

"Oh" Brian responded knowing better than to ask, "Are you a professional nurse?"

"Let's just say I'm professional."

Agent Bicks looked over towards Felker and Wex who were approaching, then looked at the woman in the revealing dark dress.

"Well, you have a peculiar way of procuring your services."

Samantha smiled proudly while sending her luggage off to her hotel. "I suppose you're right but my clients are extremely satisfied."

"I bet they are," Bicks almost whispered. "Unfortunately, I'm here on business."

"Ah" Samantha mused, "and you're one of those who doesn't like mixing business with pleasure."

"No, not really."

"Then you've definitely come to the wrong planet." Samantha sauntered away and Bicks looked after her. "Yeah, probably."

"Agent Bicks?"

The GBI agent looked the other way and saw the two detectives he was to meet up with standing nearby.

"Yes"

"I'm Felker and this is Wex."

"Yes, I recognize you from a link on my wrist-com."

Felker pointed in the direction of Samantha. "Any trouble with her?"

"Oh, there's a lot of trouble there but nothing I can't handle. This is some place."

"First visit to Maze eh?"

"Yes."

"You may want to come back when you don't have to work. Listen, I know you just got here but we have an important lead we need to follow up on and the captain would like for you to join us."

"You mean now."

The three men started walking towards the transport. Felker continued. "It's sort of like 'Game World' but much bigger, greater choices and more real."

"And apparently more dangerous." Bicks noted.

There was a moment of silence as they climbed into the transport. "Have there been any more victims since the Dubois couple?"

Felker sighed. "No inspector, you're quite up to date. However, one of our remote scanners picked up visuals of the last person seen with agent Callins, an unidentified woman."

"Yeah, we saw that too. Is that where we're going now?"

"No," Felker answered, "Her, we haven't been able to trace. Even with enhanced spectral analysis. All we know is that it is a disguised woman not wearing a wrist-com."

"I didn't think that was possible."

Wex and Felker looked at each other but Felker spoke. "Neither did we."

"So just out of curiosity,.... where are we going?"

Wex finally spoke. "To hell inspector, straight to hell."

CHAPTER 7

The family of four, Janice, Roland, their daughter Lillie and their troubled son, Bradley, got off the lift of the luxurious, Hyatt/Hilton hotel on the sixty-fourth floor. They stood on the moving platform to take them down the long, circular corridor of look-alike doors. The platform stopped in front of a numberless door which opened automatically. Evidently, everything was programmed into their wrist-coms as their luggage unlocked when they entered the rooms. Janice and Roland picked up their luggage and carried it into the master suite. Lillie rolled hers into her pink room where the walls were pre-decorated with animated Disney characters. Bradley prompted his wrist-com to take his luggage into his room. It did. Bradley was glad his parents left it up to him to design his walls in his room but also knew they would not approve of his choices. He spoke into his wrist-com and the two walls facing away from his bed, displayed new-world, planet-side, war games. The other two walls had bizarre, punk rock bands playing and singing but not loud enough to quiet the screams and roars of the war games. He could hear his dad call out "Dinner in two hours, be ready kids."

He knew he did not have to answer and heard Lillie respond. He would be ready when dinner was, and would have enough time to destroy and loot at least five villages on two worlds. Bradley was just getting started when he heard the doorbell chime. His curiosity got the best of him and he peeked out to see a maid at the door. She was small, thin, gray-haired and wore a loose gray outfit with a black apron. His parents were in robes and he could see the maid hand them a basket of fruit. Lillie was hiding behind Janice's robe as the maid spoke.

"Welcome, compliments of the management."

Bradley would be really surprised if the fruit were real but as with the rest of the family, was shocked that the maid was a real human. He crept closer. "You're human?" Janice asked.

The maid chuckled. "Yes Ma'am."

"Sorry, we've never seen a real human maid."

Bradley did not like her patronizing smile. "That's okay. This is the only hotel on Maze that still has 'em. I mean us."

Roland offered the maid credit vouchers and smiled at Janice. "Part of the great service here, I guess."

The maid stuffed the vouchers into her apron. "Thank you, I'm Clara."

"Roland Feucks and this is my wife Janice. Our daughter Lillie and Bradley, our son."

Bradley hated the fact that his father knew he was behind them listening in. He would have to study his spying program more carefully.

Meanwhile, he stepped out a bit trying to cover up his impropriety. "Hello." He said observing his father's smug smile. The maid's smile appeared more genuine when she looked at Bradley.

"Hello young man." She turned her attention back to Roland and Janice. "If you need anything at all including child care service, just mention my name on your com-link or wrist-com and I'll be here right away. Enjoy your stay."

The door closed automatically, and the maid walked away. Bradley scampered back to his room annoyed about the 'childcare service' remark but was sure it was one of the reasons his parents came here. He did not need childcare but often had to tolerate it because of his little sister. "She can babysit Lillie, not me." Bradley whispered.

His door closed and he went back to the games of mayhem and annihilation. The maid rode the moving floor of the corridor only about twenty feet and looked back to where the Feucks were. Their door was closed. She used her wrist-com to stop the moving hallway in front of another private suite. Her wrist-com had access to all the rooms and she quietly slipped in. She could hear someone working at a desk-com in their bedroom. It was a smaller residence designed for one person and in the dim light of the living room, she took off her apron and undid a few buttons on her regulation hotel blouse. Her chest expanded with the rest of her body as she filled out the uniform until it was tight-fitting. Her hair grew longer and turned red. She now looked like the cowgirl who had encountered agent Callins at the disco arena. She turned up the light, sat on a kitchen stool and started applying lipstick when a casually but well-dressed businessman in his mid-fifties walked out and was startled to see her.

"What is this? I didn't order anything!"

The maid used every move standing up slowly to exude sexual innuendo including a sultry smile. "Then perhaps you'd like to."

The businessman's voice rose to an irritating pitch. "Boy oh boy, you hookers are really getting brazen these days. Business so bad you come into people's quarters unannounced? I would have thought better of this hotel. Of course, I am assuming you work for this hotel."

He looked at her dismissively. "I haven't seen you before."

"There's a lot you haven't seen mister Chalmers and since today's your last day with us, perhaps I'll show you a few new things."

"I don't know how you got my real name but if you really did your homework, you'd know I'm not into girlie types. Furthermore, everyone knows the Harston-Olvac merger concluded this morning, subsequently, it's common knowledge that we're all leaving today. So, if you don't mind or even if you do, I think I'll just check with management to verify your employment."

Fred Chalmers, turned to walk back into his bedroom while speaking into his wrist-com.

"Management"

"Yes, may we help you?"

"I'd like to verify...."

A deep male voice spoke out. "You needn't bother, I'm not on their list". Fred looked up to see a taller well-built blonde man who was almost busting out of the hotel dress. His wrist-com spoke to him. "May we help you sir?"

The businessman almost drooled as he replied. "Uh, that's ok. Never mind." He looked up at the rogue model. "How did......"

The man stepped closer to Fred Chalmers now sitting on his bed. "I can create any form you desire."

Fred chuckled incredulously. "Wait a minute, freeze the program. Larson, you bast..."

"I'm not a program."

Fred stood up to examine the goods more closely. "What are you?"

"I'm a physimager."

Fred lightly slid his hand around certain parts of the man's body. "Physimager? I thought

they.... you were illegal."

"We are. I cost your friend Larson a bundle."

Fred smiled. "That schmuck can afford it."

"So you're not going to turn me in?" Fred's smile widened. "Maybe later."

CHAPTER 8

Candra swung the saloon doors open. She squinted at the thick cigar and cigarette smoke that greeted her but did not mind the smell of hard liquor so walked on the dirty floorboards towards the long, worn, wooden bar situated underneath a stairwell. The bartender was a short, clean-shaven man in a full length dress. He was helping a grubby gunslinger sporting an unkempt Van Dyke. The gunslinger looked over Candra with utter disgust before throwing his drink down his gullet. Candra was puzzled by the gunslinger's critical gaze and examined her own outfit. It was traditional cowboy gear: hat, boots, dirt-colored denim jeans, a silver gun in a black holster and a white shirt with a few, well placed rhinestones on it. "What can I do for you stranger?" Candra looked at the strangely attired barkeep and lowered the register in her voice. "Beer." She wanted to be taken seriously but maybe the rhinestones were a bit much.

"New in town eh? Ain't got no beer, only whisky."

"Fine." While the bartender was fetching her a drink. Candra looked around the joint. Another clean shaven short man in a slit red dress was playing an untuned piano. Four men sitting near the musician were playing cards. There were a few other men who all looked like gunslingers, smoking and drinking more than their fair share of the bar's whisky. Another clean-shaven short man in a blue satin dress with ruffles approached Candra.

"Hey handsome, buy a lonely girl a sasparilla?"

Candra almost laughed but then realized that all the men here were short and wore dresses. And upon closer examination, all the women were tall, wore beards and took on the appearance of dangerous-looking gunslingers. "Maybe some other time," she told the flirtatious short man standing next to her.

"I'll be waiting handsome."

He walked away and Candra whispered to herself. "Very funny Arnie."

"Two gelders."

Candra did not know what a gelder was but came prepared to barter. She slipped off her gold bracelet and held it up. "Will you accept this till I get to the bank?"

The bartender frowned. "What are you planning on doing, robbing it?"

Before she could object, the bartender cried out to the card players. "Hey Frank, we got us here a skip."

Frank stood up slowly. He was tall, disheveled and wore a scraggly beard. "Well, lookie here boys, a skip. A beardless one at that. Where's your beard boy?"

"Candra pretended to smile. "In my neck of the woods, we don't grow em."

"Well,.... what the hell do you grow, penises?"

All the 'men' laughed out loud for almost too long.

Candra nodded to appease them. "Look, keep the whiskey. I'm here on business. I'm looking for Madame Zulla."

"Madame Zulla? Boy, you can't even afford a drink!" This time the 'men' did laugh too long. Candra waited until the laughter died down.

"OK girls, we've all had our fun. Now how about…"

The other three men stood up and faced Candra. The all looked extremely agitated. Frank now spoke with a grimace and they all had their hands on the grip of their pistols.

"Who you calling…. girls?"

Candra realized her mistake and tried to rectify the situation and smiled weakly. "Uh, ladies?"

It did not seem possible, but the men became even more agitated. One of them stomped his foot. Another muttered incoherently. The other 'men' made room for the impending showdown by moving away from any potential gunfire and being careful to avoid any suspicion that they were involved. Frank was seething. "You know how to use that there pistol you got strapped round your waist, skip?"

Candra's smile became even more insincere. "Listen, there must be some misunderstanding. As you can plainly see, I'm not from around these parts. You're…. men, right? Yes, of course. Can't we do a little male bonding?"

The words came out of Frank's mouth very slowly. "Draw, skip."

Candra thought it might be better to negotiate. "Aw come on fella's. I just came here to look for my boyfriend, I mean, girlfriend, whatever. I tell you what, I find him, I'm outta here. What do ya say?"

The eyes on the man to Frank's right became wider. "I say he's queer Frank."

Frank did not take his eyes off Candra nor his hand from his gun. "He's dead!"

Frank almost got his gun out of its holster but crashed through the card table by a bullet from Candra's faster draw. One of the card players examined Frank. "He kill-ded Frank. Didn't even get to draw his gun properly."

The three remaining gunslingers faced Candra. They stood side by side looking at each other nervously and at Candra to see who was going to draw first. They took small steps back and apart from each other and then quickly ran out of the bar. Candra examined the other men still in the bar. They went back to the business of drinking and smoking. She turned back to the bar and quickly gulped down the large shot of whisky. The bartender watched Candra with puzzled amazement. "You outdrew Frank. Nobody's faster than Frank. You want another whiskey?"

Candra sighed. "No, like I said before, I'm looking for Madame Zulla, maybe you can tell me where I can...."

A voice came from above. "I'm Zulla. What is it you want stranger and why the hell you have to go and kill Frank for? He was my best customer."

Candra looked at the short male descending the stairs. He too was clean shaven, had on a satin black gown and was draped with jewelry from head to waist.

"He wouldn't bond." Candra responded with a smirk on her face.

"What?"

"Nevermind. I'm looking for a tall fella or girl or whatever the hell you call em around here. He has long hair and goes by the name of Byryn."

Zulla smiled and spoke to the bartender. "Babs, let me have some sherry." Zulla looked over Candra and took a sip of her sherry. "You're a good looking fella but... you want Byryn, you're gonna have to wait in line."

Candra pulled out her gun just as fast as she had done earlier. However, this time she did not fire. She just pointed her gun in Zulla's face.

"I ain't waiting in no freaking line. I just want to get the hell outta this crappy town and I'm taking him with me. Got it?"

Zulla was unimpressed and took another sip. "Yeah, I got it. The question is do you?"

"Got what?"

"Gelders. That girl cost me a lot of dough. What are you gonna offer me?

Candra holstered her gun. "How much do you want?"

"Three thousand, not a keter less."

"Done, get him ready. I won't be long."

Candra walked out of the bar. Zulla watched her leave. "What a strange one. Handsome but weird."

Babs took Candra's empty glass. "Yup, they don't come much weirder than that."

CHAPTER 9

In a lengthy, dark, tunnel, the lights of a subway transport emerged and the sound soon followed like thunder after lightning. There was only one car in the tunnel and the only passengers were special agent Bicks and detectives Felker and Wex. It was a clean, white car and the men had exhausted their conversation. Wex was looking at the darkness outside of their ride and Bicks was checking data on his wrist-com. The only sound was coming from Felker's wrist-com who was obviously enjoying his soap opera.

The transport slowed and came to a stop. Felker paused his soap and commanded his wrist-com to begin recording as the train opened its single door in the middle of the car. They stood but only saw darkness until a door slid open and their eyes strained to adjust to bright light coming from the opening. Bicks put on sunglasses and stepped into a bright, white room and his eyes could not make out any borders. Felker and Wex followed. The door closed and they could not tell where it used to be located. "So how do we get outta here?" Wex complained.

"Guess we'll worry about that later." Bicks answered calmly.

A short dark figure in a robe approached. Before he got close to them, he stopped and pointed away from them. "What the hell is he pointing at?" Asked Felker.

Nobody answered. Bicks took the lead again and walked in the direction the short figure was pointing toward. He had on a dark green robe with a hood that covered his eyes. Felker spoke quietly to Wex. "Looks like the same cat they used to have at Wonder World."

Bicks responded but did not turn back to look at him. "They have a Wonder World here?"

Felker speculated on whether Bicks had good hearing or good listening devices.

"There *was* a Wonder World here. Went outta business years ago. That is unless nobody told us it started up again which is unlikely. Hey Wex, whadya think? Maybe this is the new Wonder World."

Wex gave Felker a look telling him he was not amused and was also dreading the upcoming 'meeting' with Ozoz. "Maybe not," quipped Felker. He moved his wrist towards his mouth.

"Felker to H.Q." Mozilli's face appeared on the small screen. He looked his usual impatient self so Felker did not keep him waiting. "On our way down into the depths of Wonder World captain. This is Agent Bicks."

Agent Bicks gazed into the face of Captain Mozilli on his wrist-com.

"Pleased to meet you inspector. Sorry about the rush job to get to this site but we don't get to meet with up with Ozoz very often, in fact almost never. I know you've come a long way but you'll get to rest up after the meeting." The expression on Bicks face indicated that something was finally bothering him. "No problem captain. Glad I'm able to assist but.... I have no information about this.... Ozoz character."

Mozilli sighed. "That's because we know next to nothing about him or 'it.' What I can tell you is that he is non-human, is somehow connected to the planet Maze and has powers we have yet to determine."

"And he's a potential perpetrator in this case." added Bicks.

"An unlikely scenario. As far as we can tell, he's never left the area you're going to. He actually wanted to meet up with us about this case and we're granting his request,…. carefully."

The small, robed individual stopped, and the three men did as well.

"Anyway, my team and MazeCor are all looking forward to working with you. Welcome to Maze agent Bicks. Mozilli out."

Before Bicks could respond, another door opened into utter darkness.

Their host directed them towards the darkness and Bicks walked in. Felker and Wex commanded their wrist-coms to produce light and they did so to reveal a square room with no features. Wex gasped as the floor lowered and the men were plummeting at a rapid rate. Felker looked at the specs on his wrist-com. "Approaching one hectometer below the surface, heading due north…. uh oh."

The lights on their wrist-coms went out and the men were once again in darkness. They could feel the elevator plummeting rapidly and Wex leaned back against where he remembered the wall was. Felker directed his comments towards Bicks. "I believe this is about the same place communications dropped the last time someone visited Ozoz."

"When was that?" Asked Bicks.

"Several years ago. Our former captain was the one who visited him."

"Looks like he didn't have much to say about Ozoz."

Felker paused for a moment. "No, he resigned after that visit. We don't talk about it much."

The men could feel the elevator slow its descent and come to a stop. A door opened again and they got out into another very bright, white room. The door closed and the short, robed guide was not with them. Again there was no sign of where the elevator was nor any sign of the perimeter of where they now were. Felker slowly turned around. "So, where do we go from here?"

The men appeared disconcerted but did not have to wait long for an answer. A low voice that sounded male and female with a slight echo enveloped the room. "Stop, do not come any closer."

Felker and agent Bicks looked around trying to guess where they thought the voice might be emanating from. Wex retreated quickly from where he thought it might be.

CHAPTER 10

The wall behind Phillimus Mekkel's office desk had become a screen. The screen was divided into twenty-five sections and in twenty-two of the equally divided sections were mostly human- looking heads of MazeCor representatives. A few of the heads resembled some other species. Three of the divided sections had 'absent' spelled out diagonally across them. In the middle of the screen, a member of an outside investment group was speaking and because of that, her head was marginally enlarged.

"In view of the current unstable market and in an attempt secure profitability in the Valluk-Prine region, the Holst Group is re-negotiating its limited partnership with the intent to expand to a general partnership." Phillimus looked back at Kelde who was a few feet away and spoke softly. "Here it comes."

The lawyer from the Holst Group continued. "This general partnership is conditional on the dissolution of the MazeCor limited partnership." Several people started talking at once but the lawyer regained control. "Let me finish, please. With the dissolution of both limited partnerships, representative shareholders would now become general partners in an expanded tri-regional conglomerate. Based on statistics which are now being sent to you, you can readily ascertain the benefits of this merger. This offer will stand for thirty days. A quorum of twenty representatives must agree to the conditions of the merger and general partnership by the end of the thirty days. A rough draft of the terms of the merger are available by pressing 'star one' on your desk-com."

Once again, all the representatives wanted to speak but Phillimus Mekkel's cat-like face appeared where the lawyer's had been. "Representatives, we have been approached by outside interests because we seem to be vulnerable at the moment and consequently our share values have decreased. Now, while there is a potentially critical situation on the Pleasure Planet, you will also notice in our shareholders report the tourist index has not changed. I repeat, unchanged. Which also means that the profit margin has also not changed. So, what is the share depreciation based on, speculation? As you well know, I am not one to stand in the way of progress, however, since you do have thirty days to decide whether or not to join in a tempting but unproven general tri-regional partnership, I recommend reconvening and assessing the situation at that time."

Mekkel's face faded from view and was replaced by Cronus Aberpratny, the vice-chair of MazeCor. He was an older man who had an affected way of speaking and dressing.

"The vice chair concurs with the chairman. All in favor of adjourning and reconvening in thirty days to respond to said motion please press star three."

Cronus gave the members time to respond on their com-links. "Thank you, all opposed?

Thank you. The ayes have it and the motion is carried. We will reconvene at S.D. 46.15 . This meeting is now adjourned."

The wall returned to its normal brown color in Mekkel's office. He and Kelde sat there in the semi-dark momentarily reflecting on what had just transpired.

"I think you accomplished what you needed to." Kelde suggested.

Phillimus grimaced. "Buying us some time? Perhaps. If the tourist index drops and subsequently ensues a share loss, we'll be having that meeting long before thirty days."

Kelde nodded in agreement. Mekkel sat up in his chair and looked at his desk com.

"Are we still in contact with the detectives?"

Kelde smiled out of habit. "No, lost them at 22.10 in the exact location we lost our former police captain."

"Wherever the hell that was. At least Ozoz is consistent. What about Mozilli?"

Kelde's smile gained more credibility. "On his way over."

"Good" Mekkel said as he rose, "I'll be in the whirlpool. Let me know when he arrives and I'll take my time getting out."

"Mind if I order some victuals?"

"Already ordered. Have a drink while you're waiting."

Phillimus Mekkel entered his personal spa. Kelde could see the eight, even-fingered massage bot hand him a towel before the door closed. Kelde knew he would always be Mekkel's hand, but he would never replace him as chairman of MazeCor. The only reason Mekkel was still chairman after four years, was because no one would tolerate Cronus Aberpratny. The vice chair's feigned importance was exacerbated by the tone of his voice. There were too many times during a business meeting when Mekkel had to reign him in. On one occasion, Kelde had suggested to Mekkel that he send Aberpratny to visit Ozoz. Mekkel smiled but Kelde knew he seriously considered the idea. No one would mind. Kelde swiveled in his chair to face the beverage dispenser and requested the usual.

"Gin and tonic on the rocks."

He removed the drink from the dispenser and took a big gulp. He thought that perhaps the perks were more appealing than they should be and the underlying reason why he did not want to alter his employment. After he took his second gulp, he knew there was no doubt.

CHAPTER 11

The sound of sobbing was coming out of Fred Chalmers bedroom. Dressed in a robe, he grabbed a glass of water from the kitchen dispensary and headed to where the sound was coming from. The physimager, dressed as a male maid, was sitting on the bed half out of his ill-fitting dress and crying. Fred handed him the water. "I can't believe you're sitting there feeling sorry for yourself. You're one of the most incredible creatures in the known universe and you'd rather be human? Kos! I wish I could trade places with you. I spend all my time, when I have time, in Lillum tanks trying to avoid humans. You have no idea!" Fred sat on the other side of the bed facing away from the maid. "Listen, I gotta get some sleep." "I have a pretty intense program on the way back to Siddum 5. You can sleep here but you'll have to crash on the couch."

The physimager wiped the runny make-up and tears from his face and lay next to Fred.

"You really want to be like one of us?"

The businessman sat up excited. "You can do that?"

"I believe so."

"What do I need to do? I'll pay you whatever."

"Just lie still, close your eyes and concentrate on what you'd really like to be."

"I'll do it. I'll do it."

Fred Chalmers lay back down and closed his eyes. He was giddy thinking about the possibilities of being someone who could change his appearance at will and all the advantages he would have working in the newly formed business merger. He could grow his hair back, have an amazing sex life and finally beat Larson at racquetball. He laughed out loud thinking about it. He felt himself grow, getting stronger and more alien- like, changing into a few versions of himself. It was an exhilarating sensation like sex but even better. He cried out with glee and could not contain his excitement so opened his eyes and screamed at what had become of his body. He had become joined with a giant luminous slug with a woman's head. Four antennae coming from the side of her head were waving wildly. She opened her mouth in a ghastly smile to reveal rows of small, round and sharp teeth. Two tentacles grew out of her and linked themselves into Fred's arms as she pulled his torso and then his head into her until his screams could no longer be heard. And as if to answer his screams she quietly uttered. "I guess it didn't work."

When Fred was completely dissolved into her, the physimager returned to her original maid form. She held up the damaged dress and put it back on as best she could. She looked around the now quiet room and before leaving could hear the desk-com calling for Fred Chalmers.

She walked back into the bedroom already changed into the form of Fred and asked "Yes?"

"Are you all right, sir?" The metallic voiced machine inquired. "We heard some strange noises."

"Oh yes, yes, everything's fine. Just having a little fun."

"Very good sir. Please continue to do so and sorry for the interruption." The desk-com service monitor chimed out and was replaced with stat sheets from Fred's work. "Oh, what a dull boy. Time to go out on the town, Fred."

The physimager destroyed the maid's wrist-com she "borrowed" and slipped on the businessman's. She then selected one of Fred's nicer suits with a matching shirt. Picking out a contrasting tie, she put it all on and looked in the mirror deciding Fred would look better with a full head of hair, grew it, and walked out the door.

CHAPTER 12

The wooden floor creaked as Candra stepped inside the dirty-white painted bank. A manager of some sort was smoking a cigar that smelled like burning grass. He was short like all the men here, Candra thought, or women correcting herself, and had on a plain black dress. There were no customers in the bank. There was a dog sleeping near the teller and the teller appeared to be in the same condition. The manager smiled showing a few gold teeth behind a poor choice of red lipstick. "Good morning. Would you like to open an account with us today?" The teller and dog woke at the same time. "No," Candra replied, "I'm just making a withdrawal."

"A withdrawal?" The manager repeated turning her smile into a frown, "I don't believe I've seen you here before."

"Yeah, I'm from out of town but I arranged to transfer funds to this bank."

"Oh really?" The bank manager stood up smiling again. "And what name would the transferred funds be listed under?"

Candra tried to hide the fact that she had to get that information from Arnie. She spoke in a whisper while rubbing her neck. "Arnie, what name do I use?"

"Calamity Jane." Candra repeated the name not expecting the look of terror on the banker's face. However, it did have the desired effect. The manager looked at Candra in awe and repeated her name slowly. "Calamity Jane, yes Sir, I'll take care of that personally." The manager keyed the door and rushed behind the partition to take the teller's place.

"Yes, I see you have a credit of two-thousand, seven-hundred, twenty-nine gelders and fifty-three keters. How much of that would you like to withdraw today?"

Candra whispered again. "Damn it!" She could see that the banker was frightened of her and used a gentler tone. "I'm sorry, there must be some mistake. I should have *twenty*-two thousand seven-hundred twenty-nine dollars, I mean gelders and fifty-three keters. Could you take another look? Please." The banker looked at his ledger and shook her head and the teller joined in on the head shaking.

"Sorry sir, our records indicate two-thousand-seven-hundred, twenty- ..."

"Ok, fine!" Candra's modest outburst caused the manager and teller to step back. "I'll check with my sources and return momentarily."

"That'll be fine sir." The banker said grinning, watching her leave.

As soon as she closed the door to the bank, Candra raised her wrist-com near her mouth,

"Kos dammit Arnie, what the hell?"

Arnie took on the appearance of a fat banker dressed in a pin-striped, navy blue suit. His back was facing Chandra and he swiveled around in an old wooden chair to face her.

He spoke with a southern U.S. drawl. "Yes, sugar baby? What can sugar *daddy* do for you?"

"You know damn well what you can do."

"Ooooh, short on funds are we?"

"Arnie!"

"Well, I'm sure we can come to some sort of loan agreement."

"WHAT?"

"Let's see, twenty-thousand gelders at a sixteen percent interest rate,... oh my! You're gonna owe our little company twenty-three thousand gelders."

"I'm gonna owe your little company a program wipe."

"My, oh my, I do believe that remark could cost you even more money in a civil lawsuit."

"Cut the crap Arnie! Transfer the funds!"

Arnie dropped the accent. "Nasty, just nasty. It's done."

Candra headed back to the bank. "Thank you. And who the hell is Calamity Jane?"

Arnie laughed. "I'll let you figure that one out. And oh, by the way, I am taking my interest and fees out of those Balkin red credits."

The branch manager and his teller slowly counted the money three times and Candra was out of the bank in forty minutes. She knew she would be approaching Maze soon and needed to get out of the ship's Lillum tank. She swung open the doors to the saloon and walked up to the bar. The same men with the obvious exception of Frank, were playing cards and smoking rolled ciga-rettes. The piano player was the only one who ignored Candra. Zulla was sitting with Frank's boys and saw their agitation. "Easy boys. This shouldn't take long." She walked up to the bar as Candra plopped a satchel on top of it and pulled stacks of bills out.

"Three-thousand gelders, where is he,... er,... she?"

"I'll go up and get her ready. Why don't you relax and have a drink on me, and,.... keep your gun holstered please."

Madam Zulla climbed the stairs and Babs poured Candra a whisky. She turned to look at Frank's boys and they turned back to their card game. Candra lifted the glass to her lips but nothing came out. The drink was frozen in place. There was no piano music and everyone in the bar was immobile.

"What's up Arnie?"

This time only Arnie's voice came through. "Approaching Maze, E.T.A. one hour, forty-seven minutes. Netting will commence in thirty-two minutes without incident, sooner with."

"Thanks Arnie. I'll get dressed planetside. Resume program."

Candra returned to her whisky just as it started to fall. She grabbed the glass and consumed the beverage. The music began again as well as the 'men' playing cards and smoking. Byryn walked behind Madame Zulla from the top of the stairs. He was clean shaven, wore nothing but a slip and makeup. He also was highly intoxicated and singing an incomprehensible song. Candra looked up at him.

"You're in fine shape for traveling. Madame Zulla, how much for your best room?"

"Twenty-five, bath included."

"Done." Candra started ascending the stairs as Zulla came down. "Send up a strong pot of coffee and find him, her, some decent clothing."

"That'll be extra."

"Whatever, just bring it." Byryn stumbled but opened the door to the room he had just left.

Candra watched him bemused. "I thought we got you a better singing program."

Byryn started to reel and Candra caught him and laid him on the red velvet bedspread.

The bedspread matched the curtains and went well with the dark mahogany in the room. Candra took off her gun belt and tossed her hat to the side while Byryn continued to sing in bed. "Drunk as a skunk, Kos, I can't believe you let them do this to you. You have got to do better than this buddy boy,..... Kos! You look sexy!"

Candra undid a few buttons on her shirt and lay next to Byryn. "So, how many tricks did you turn?"

Byryn stopped singing. "Oh, bout two,... three,..... hundred." He laughed and Candra joined in.

"Wait, really?" They both laughed again and Candra kissed Byryn on the mouth. The kiss did not last long as Byryn and everything in the room vanished. Candra's outfit turned into expanding blue foam. "ARNIE! That was not thirty-two minutes!"

Arnie's face appeared with an airline pilot's hat on. "Sorry lambkins. Rotor foil shaft defaulted entering atmosphere. Will initiate repair planetside. Just taking necessary precautions."

"Yeah, well your timing sucks!"

"Well excuse me while I try to save your complaining narrow ass."

The blue foam filled the Lillum tank. There was a bubble of space around Candra's face that created a screen for her to observe the ships outer cameras and the LED read outs monitoring the ship. The read-outs became blurry as the ship started to vibrate. Outside of the ship, Candra could see the mandibles retracting and the hull become bright red due to the heat upon entering Maze's atmosphere.

CHAPTER 13

After Wex had fled the immediate area and disappeared into the bright white, Felker immediately drew his gun and it flew out of his hands. Bicks looked up and around. "We are here for Ozoz. I am agent Bicks...."

"I am Ozoz. I know who you are. There is one missing."

There was a long scream and presently, Wex was back with them. His pants were wet.

"Now we are complete."

All three men looked for the location of where the voice was coming from, but it was ubiquitous.

"The creature you are looking for, cannot be apprehended by you. Your only chance to eliminate it, is to bring it here to me. You agent Bicks, will be the lure."

Agent Bicks cleared his voice. "Wait,.....you sent for me?"

"In a covert manner."

"Well, it's nice to know who I'm working for. You said creature."

The physimager. A San-gli Torran shape shifter, unknown to most humanoids in this space sector."

"So how do I find this physimager?"

"You do not. It will find you as will your protection. Which, hopefully, will reach you before the shape shifter does.

"My protection?"

"You will need it."

"No doubt. Providing this is true, why are you helping us eliminate this creature?"

"Truth is limited by perception and in that regard, your species is nearly blind. But know this, this creature usurps my position. I will not allow it."

"And just what exactly is your position?"

"Why an amusement, not unlike yourself. For many years I was the main attraction on this planet."

Felker spoke quietly to Bicks. "Yeah, until people started to disappear."

"Those individuals fulfilled their destiny in this space time just as the physimager approaches hers."

Felker spoke quietly again. "It's a she?"

"It is more female than male but then again, so are you. You just can't do anything about it. This interview is over. Go back the way you came."

The men stood there quietly for a moment until Bicks spoke up. "Why don't you show yourself?"

There was another pause and the strange voice sounded out again. "You would not survive the viewing. Your guide awaits you."

The men turned to see the short, robed figure waiting for them. They followed him in the undefined whiteness until a door opened where they got on a dark elevator. As the lift ascended, their wrist-coms reactivated. Felker looked at Wex in the dim light provided by their wrist-coms and smiled wryly. "Well ol pal. We survived Ozoz." Wex did not respond. When the elevator stopped. The door opened and there was the singular subway car waiting for them. The guide was nowhere in sight and the men climbed onto the car. Felker signaled Mozilli. "The 'interview' is over captain, we're heading back to the station."

Mozilli smiled on Felker's wrist-com. "Well, well, looks like Ozoz is not so disagreeable after all. I'll see you when you get back."

Mozilli faded out and Felker returned to his favorite soap opera as the three men rode the quiet car back to the populace of Maze and police headquarters.

CHAPTER 14

A red door approximately ten feet high slid open. Inside was a monster sleeping in a space it was too large for. It had horns all over its dark green body and arms that looked like its legs. The creature had a nose that protruded too much, situated between its closed eyes and similar slits on its face oozing white liquid. Between snores, its extremely wide mouth barely opened to reveal dozens of crooked, red teeth. It smelled worse than it looked.

Realizing that they had opened the wrong door, the Feucks family backed away from the large, unpleasant looking, stinking beast. Before they got more than a dozen feet away, the creature woke up, saw them and began growling in a threatening manner. Roland thought it best to close the door immediately, ran back and closed it. The creature began pounding on the metal door as the family ran down a corridor lined with small plants that tried to bite whatever got too close. Looking back, they knew it was a brief matter of time before the door came down. At the end of the corridor in the large game room, there were three similar red doors. "Which door?" Bradley yelled. One of the three doors started to get pounded from the inside out. Lillie screamed.

"Not that one!" Roland Feucks answered hoping his children were enjoying this reality game adventure, however, they all looked scared. Roland opened one of the other doors and behind it was a blue sky with clouds scattered about and no landing in sight. The other door was locked. "We have to jump!"

Janice looked at Roland wide-eyed. "Are you crazy!?"

The monster at the end of the corridor broke through the door.

Lillie screamed again and Janice tried to comfort her. "It's not going to eat us darling, it's just a game."

Roland was watching the monster get closer to them. "A program that will be over if we don't keep moving. Brad what are you doing?"

"Looking for a key. There's always a key hidden somewhere. Uh oh."

The monster was upon them and drooling over the meal it would make of the family. It let out a terrible growl-like scream and as it did, the second door was broken through by another monster that looked and stank even worse than the first. The two monsters sized each other up, got on all fours and roared at each other before battling over who got to eat the family.

"Found it!" Bradley held up a key he found hidden in a small green biting shrub that only managed to bite him twice. There was no blood drawn.

"Good job son." Roland took the key and fumbled with it while the monsters halted their attack on each other and stood up to each other. One of them growled in recognition of the other and the other monster smiled in its own horrible way. The two creatures walked towards each other and hugged like they were long lost siblings. Tongues that looked like thick, black rope dripping oil, protruded out and the creatures licked each other. "That's disgusting," said Janice reacting to their overt affection. And as if they heard her, the monsters turned towards the family growling and baring oversized red teeth.

"DAD!" Brad yelled.

"Got it!" Roland proclaimed victoriously. He swung the door open and the family rushed into a room where there was no light.

"What do we do now?" Asked Janice.

"Well we can't stay here," said Roland responding to the sound of the door being pounded through.

He knew that his son had played this game before on a screen in Game World and felt reluctant, but asked him for his advice. "Bradley?"

"We have to find another door!" Bradley answered. They spread out desperately searching until they heard Lillie's scream and saw the monsters burst through the door. Light coming through the bashed in door allowed Roland to see another door and he yelled "Here!"

The four humans rushed to the door, but it would not open.

"Use the key," yelled Janice. "There's no lock! Maybe it's a voice command," answered Roland desperately. All four yelled "Open!" It did not work and the monsters were almost upon them. Roland looked at his son, but he just shrugged. "Lillie, you try."

Lillie yelled "open!" and the door did as she commanded. Once again, there was a blue sky before them with no place to land. "I guess we should have jumped before" said Roland, "let's go."

There was no argument from the other family members. They held hands and jumped before the monsters were able to get to them.

Lillie screamed but moments later, they were softly caught in a cloud that lowered them into a small vehicle for four.

Janice smiled, relieved and looked at the children. Lillie was as wild-eyed as ever and Bradley looked like he was bored. Things were normal. "I guess this program is over" she said.

Roland returned her gaze at him. "Yeah, I guess so."

"Finally" Bradley quietly stated.

The wind revealed they were moving and before Bradley could guess what mode of transportation they were in, the vehicle became a roller coaster and took a steep dive with no end in sight. This time, they all screamed.

CHAPTER 15

Mozilli got off the private elevator facing the door of the MazeCor chairman. He looked at the heading and paused before entering, knowing it was going to be an unpleasant meeting. He sighed and opened the door. It was dark as usual, the way Phillimus Mekkel liked it. The chairman's wide leather seat was empty. Kelde, another individual who added to the unpleasantness in manner and looks was sitting against the wall drinking something that smelled like it would petrify most internal organs. Mozilli smiled at that idea and could see that Kelde was wearing a smirk in preparation for the dreadful meeting.

"He'll be right out." Kelde said, his words somewhat slurred as usual. "Have a seat."

There was only one place for Mozilli to sit, close to and in front of Mekkel's desk.

Mozilli sat facing away from Kelde and decided that he might as well start in with the unpleasantries as he sat in the uncomfortable chair. "You don't age do you Kelde? I mean, you look like shit, but you don't age. Amazing."

"Your sense of humor is about as satisfying as your investigation, Mo."

It was Mekkel coming through the door from his private spa.

"We can do better."

"I guess you will now that you have a member of the GBI on your team. I think you know that we wanted to avoid any notoriety outside of our influence about our visitor who has a bad habit of eating our tourists. But it seems Ozoz has other plans."

"Yes" Mozilli added, "Agent Bicks himself didn't know Ozoz was the reason he was here nor was he aware that Ozoz would be providing protection for him. He did say however, that he would have no problem keeping this out of circulation."

Mekkel furry eyebrows raised. "Protection?"

"Ozoz didn't elaborate on that. Guess we'll find out as the investigation proceeds."

Mekkel leaned back in his chair. "So much for keeping this out of circulation."

Mozilli did not know how to respond so he just shrugged.

"You're a clever detective captain. I am sure by now you realize that if word gets out about our terrible little secret; people disappearing, leaving only a hat or a shoe, stockholders get nervous. Shares lose value. Somebody says, "we've got to do something" and before you know it, my job is on the line, and so is Kelde's. Of course, your head is rolling well ahead of ours because that's the way things work here at MazCor, right? Someone always has to be the fall guy. But I didn't need to bring you here just to tell you something I could have called you about. Then again, I wouldn't have been able to see those tiny little hairs on the back of your neck stand up, now would I?"

Phillimus Mekkel knew better than to wait for an answer to the rhetorical question. He moved on to a more practical question. "So captain, have you come up with some plan to capture this blessed creature before we all lose what we can't afford to?"

Mozilli had no real plan. The GBI agent, Brian Bicks, had told him that they would have to rely on 'good ol detective work.' That remark disappointed him, but realistically, they both knew that their best hope of solving this case was the mysterious entity Ozoz . The captain did not want to relay that thought to Mekkel. He lied. "We're going to put out two dozen decoys, androids, to bait the creature and increase drone surveillance by 150%. We don't want to alarm the tourist, but we're going to include 'suggestions' in our general welcome statement to warn visitors against anything not a part of their general programing or anyone not wearing a wrist-com. That's what we've implemented so far."

Mozilli could tell by Mekkel's facial expression, he thought this plan was too little beyond standard protocol. He also knew the MazeCor head would have a long list of standard suggestions and recommendations. Things he had heard too many times before, but that Mekkel would enjoy repeating to him, slowly. That did not bother Mozilli very much. What really annoyed him was that he knew Kelde was sitting behind him enjoying every moment. He was exhausted by the time he got out of Mekkel's office. He could hear the festive horns and Zydeco music of Mardi Gras a few blocks away. In this part of the city, Mardi Gras was the first week of every month. As he strode down the steps away from the entryway of the MazeCor skyscraper, he unwrapped a Tylenol lolly. He had already signaled for an auto-cab and one was pulling up curbside. "Police headquarters" he said climbing into the cab. The self-driving cab took off and Mozilli could see the parade on a side street. He looked for the surveillance drones and the auto-cops but did not see any. Mozilli decided to relax. He knew the police equipment was in place and its veiled operation to expose the monster in their midst would fail. Ozoz told Bicks that only he could induce that creature. Mozilli was okay with that plan. He just hoped that not too many tourists would disappear before this case was solved because Mekkel was right. He would be the fall guy and people still cheered when the figurative head was chopped off.

CHAPTER 16

Inside of the bubble shower with her eyes closed, Candra held on to the grips and let the powerful spray remove the last remnants of the self-dissolving blue foam. When that was accomplished, the water jets became air jets and dried her off quickly. She put on a shark-skin slip watching the monitors show the repair-droids repair the mandibles on the exterior of her ship. They had landed in a secluded area for emergency situations. Arnie did not think it was an emergency but was directed to land there regardless. He obliged but not without complaining. Candra also scanned images of Maze to see what kind of world she had landed on. "Hmm, looks like a good time but some people get to have fun, and some get to work."

Candra dressed in her usual garb; a short chain-mail dress, sneaker boots, a wrist-com and finally, a backpack. "Arnie?"

Arnie popped into view. He had the usual nose and mouth but only one eye. It was abnormally large and had a horn above it. "What do you think?" He asked.

"Oh Kos! Open the forward hatch please."

"Yes, Ma'am" he said, pleased with his new look.

The forward hatch opened and Candra stepped out. She would have to go through customs before finding her way to a Betan trade merchant. It was a pleasant day, but she had seen on the ships com that the weather was always pleasant here. Maze was not going to lose any customers because of bad weather. A small hovercraft was waiting to take her to customs and getting in, she noticed she was the only one in the ride. On the way to customs, she saw other spacecraft being repaired. One, in the distance, was burning and several fire-bots were trying to contain the flames.

Candra's transport came to a halt slowly. A servo-bot rolled up. It looked like all the other bots servicing the spaceport; short with a cylindrical white metallic body and a button shaped head slightly larger than its neck. It had one lighted green eye and a speaker below and spoke in an accent that sounded like French mixed with Spanish. "Papers please."

"Papers?" Candra repeated and thought, how antiquated. She raised her arm. "How about a wrist com?"

"Wrist-com, wrist-com, wrist-com,.... no papers?"

"Nope, no papers, just a wrist-com."

The servo-bot repeated what she said like it was talking to itself and shook its head rapidly.

There was buzzing and something that sounded like a mechanical duck coming out of its speaker's mouth. Finally, it spoke again "papers please."

Candra sighed, "Arnie, can you link with this thing?"

Arnie popped onto Candra's wrist-com looking like a cheap female version of the servo-bot.

He used a sexy voice. "I'll try."

There was more buzzing and duck noise coming from the servo-bot. This time its head shook violently and fell to one side. A rod with a flashing red light emerged from the neck and the servo-bot was motionless.

"Arnie! You weren't supposed to break it!"

"I did nothing. It is a useless piece of junk."

"Can you fix it? We can't go anywhere until this bot is operational again."

"Ha! Now you know darn well that tampering with a space shuttle servo-bot is against the law and is punishable by a hefty fine and possible lengthy detainment. But you'll be the one detained. I'll be back in the comfort of the ship."

"So, what the Kos are we supposed to do, just sit here?"

Before Arnie could answer, a small robot that looked like a tricycle with a head approached.

It changed into a walking bot. A flexible arm grew out and it turned the red light off on the servo-bot.

"Ahh, a bot repairing-bot." Candra said to herself.

The repair-bot spoke in a monotonous voice. "Repairs being made, please keep a respectable distance from the work area. Thank you."

"What's wrong with it?" Candra asked.

"Outdated model. Too many repairs required."

"I told you!" Arnie piped in.

Candra ignored him and spoke to the repair-bot who had now grown a few more arms with pneumatic tools attached to them. "So why don't they buy new ones?"

The repair-bot sounded bored. "It's union. It would cost them too much to get rid of it."

The pole on the servo-bot receded and the repair-bot closed its head back. "Work completed, please wait momentarily for servo-bot to accommodate you. Thank you and sorry for the inconvenience."

The repair-bot turned into a tricycle with a head again and sped off. The green light on the servo-bot came back on and it spoke again.

"Papers please."

"Oh Kos" Candra responded in an exhausted manner as she heard Arnie's annoying laugh come out of her wrist-com.

CHAPTER 17

The sun was glistening off Blackwater Lake. The water was still and calm but ripples started forming as a hovercraft approached the dock. With his permanent smile, the skipper-bot turned his head almost 180 degrees and spoke to the passengers. "Maze Labyrinth, largest labyrinth on twenty-four worlds. Fifteen entrances and endless adventure. Caution is recommended as well as traveling with a robo-guide available by way of your wrist-com. Enjoy! Next departure in twenty minutes."

Samantha and the other five passengers walked off the vessel and stepped onto a platform. The platform looked like a raft with thick velvet ropes on all four sides. It moved quietly away from the wind turbines of the hovercraft and parked at a ramp while the passengers all looked at their wrist-coms directing them to their pre-determined entry points. Tourists who had left previous transports, minutes, days or weeks earlier, managed to find their way back to this location and were waiting to board the returning platform. The last ones to get on before it departed were Silvia and Mel. They were both out of breath and Silvia spoke to Mel. "What were we thinking?" From a bent over position breathing heavily, Mel just nodded and smiled.

One of the entrances to the labyrinth was a giant human face. It was a man's angry face, bald and showing lots of teeth. Since Samantha had not made a choice, she decided that this was the one for her. Also, the description on her wrist-com said that walking through this entrance was one of the more adventurous and dangerous choices. "Right up my alley" she mused. She smiled and swung open the bottom gate-like middle tooth and walked through alone.

CHAPTER 18

The Mardi Gras parade was over two miles long. This month's theme was Earth Deities and there were seventy floats representing many of Earth's renowned god's and goddesses. Elliot, the sweeper from the space shuttle and his blond girlfriend, Cindi, were on top of a float. Cindi stood in the middle of the float in a costume that resembled a mountain. Her hat, which was supplied by the bottom part of her costume would erupt candy and beads every so often to simulate a volcanic explosion. She was representing the Hawaiian goddess Pele and was supposed to wave her arms at the crowds but was preoccupied watching Elliot and five mostly undressed female Hulu dancers dancing around her. She tried aiming the hard candy at Elliot's head but the costume was too rigid. From her heightened vantage point Cindi could see the casinos and a tall woman in a chain mail dress with color matched sneaker boots and backpack walk into one. She thought about the woman getting a tall cool beverage and wished she were her, especially since the volcano she was wearing was a little too warm and also, the man who was supposed to keep her thirst abated, Elliot, was preoccupied.

Candra walked into a casino that was two city blocks long and just as wide. She could not help but notice the loud whoops of joy and excitement from people all over the playing area. She was accosted by a large and sexy robo-server who did not move his legs. He was on some kind of rollers. "Would you like a beverage?" He asked. Candra was not thirsty but did not feel like turning him away so soon. "I'll take a vodka tonic." "Really?" It was Arnie with a disapproving look on his face. Candra ignored her wrist-com. The robo-servers midriff slid open and after it dispensed her drink, he reached in and gave it to Candra. She waited for him to tell her the cost but he simply whirled away while checking on other customers. "Waiter, gaming supervisor and security all wrapped up in one." Candra quietly mentioned as the robo-server rolled away.

"I'm not impressed." Arnie said. "It's only a level three robo."

"Whelp, that's two levels higher than you."

A laughing chimpanzee's face appeared on her wrist-com and then Arnie's face came back.

"That's not funny."

Candra tried the drink. "Whew! That is strong!

Arnie ignored her complaint. "The service rep is to your left behind the roulette tables."

Candra frowned. "Who told you I was looking for a service rep?"

Arnie took on the appearance of an elderly woman with a hand on her hip. "Honey, please!"

Candra almost laughed but thought better. She took another sip and placed the drink at a gaming table before reaching the service rep. He was dressed smartly, had a streak of white in his black hair and was sipping on a colorful drink. He smiled wryly as Candra approached him.

"May I help you?"

Candra looked surprised. "You're human!"

"As far as I know. You can always tell who the robo's are. They're all white." The service rep chuckled slightly. "Now what can I do for you?"

Candra looked around. "People win a lot here."

The service rep's smile broadened. "People come here to win so we let them."

"So how do you stay in business?"

"We don't let them win that much. Believe it or not, they would get bored and would not come back. The challenge is always about winning."

"I see." Candra smiled broadly and leaned slightly towards him. "How can I get a line of credit?"

The service rep also leaned slightly forward while checking out her voluptuous form. "From me or from the house?"

It was Candra's turn to chuckle slightly. "From the house."

The service rep leaned back. "Damn. What's your name?"

"Candra, with a C."

"That's it?"

"That's it."

"Okay. My names Randall, Candra with a C. Let's see what's available." Randall spoke into his wrist-com. "Credit evaluation for Candra with a C. Hmm, twenty-three Candra's with a C. All with last names. Wait, did you just come here from the *Yarr* Sector?"

"Oh no, of course not. That's illegal isn't it?"

"Yes, and you don't look like the legal type."

"Well, hypothetically, if I were from that sector, what then?"

"Then you'd have a credit line of two-hundred and forty-five thousand. Before penalties of course."

"What kind of penalties are we talking about?"

"Through the house or,...... ?"

"Let's go through you this time."

"Ten percent."

"Whew, that's a nice cut,..... for you."

"The House gets 25. Then again, I *could* make it a better deal for you."

"I bet you could. Is your boss aware of your wheeling's and dealings?"

"Of course, he gets a cut as well."

"So why don't I just go with the 'House'?"

"You can but you should know, the 'House' transaction gets reported."

"Ah, I see. I guess we don't want that."

"Would you like to hear the better deal from yours truly?"

"No, I'll settle on the ten percent cut."

"It involves me buying you dinner."

"Thank you. I appreciate the offer, but I have other plans."

The service rep nodded slightly. "I bet you do. I'll need to link with your ships com."

"Of course. Arnie..."

From her wrist-com, Earth's Far Eastern mystical music came out and Candra could see several Arabic belly dancers circle dance around a column of smoke which turned into Arnie. A booming voice was heard, and Arnie appeared as a genie with a green face with long pointed ears and a similar nose. "Who has summoned the great Al Baheem Basharee?"

Candra shook her head. "Cut the crap and link the ships com to this casino."

"It is done my Princess and because of my renown munificence, the great Al Baheem Basharee has granted you two more wishes."

"Good, stop with the faces and get lost."

"Humph! In his very presence you dare insult the great Al Beheem..."

Candra moved her wrist-com closer to her face. "Arnie, read my lips... GET LOST!"

Arnie almost yelled back at her. "I shall and you'll be sorry!"

Randall slid his fingers across his desk-com screen. "Trouble with your ships com?"

Candra did not respond. "Okay." the service rep continued looking up from his desk-com.

"That leaves you a balance of two-hundred, twenty-thousand and five-hundred credits. I just need a voice confirmation to seal this transaction." Randall held his wrist-com close to Candra and she responded. "Candra"

"Very good. You are all set. Is there anything else I can do for you?"

Candra eyed Randall carefully before speaking. "Yes, there is. Where can I find a Betan Trade Merchant?"

Randall's eyebrows raised. "Ho, ho, ho. Now you're really beginning to look illegal." "Would a few credits make me look more legal?"

"A few?"

"Thousand."

A big smile came across Randall's face. "You're starting to look more and more legal by the minute. It's absolutely amazing. Ok, you're all set. Your wrist-com will direct you to the party you seek."

Candra smiled, pleased with the service. "There *is* something else I need to know."

Randall's smile got bigger before he spoke. "Is this the part where you ask me what time I get off work?"

"Not exactly." Randall's smile became a pout. "Do you know anything about Ozoz?"

Any hint of humor became lost on Randall's face. "WHAT?" He looked around. "Don't even say that,.. that name out loud. Ha, no! Forget about that."

"Why? What's the problem?"

"The problem? Listen, you're new here and someone's playing a bad joke on you. Very bad. People who go looking for that dude,... you never see em again. You know what I'm saying? Whiit! Find that cat, noooo come back. You hear me?" Randall's smile came back.

"Now, why don't you just run along, have some fun cause this is definitely the place for that. And, if you need any help spending some of those credits, you know where to find me."

Candra stared at Randall for a brief while. "Ok, Thanks for your help." She then turned and walked out of the casino.

CHAPTER 19

At the end of a long pier, a large yacht was partially hidden behind fog. Samantha walked slowly along the pier listening to the water and the party sounds coming from the ship. As she approached the ramp, several voices could be heard as well as the distinct singing voice of Sting. At the top of the ramp, there was a velvet rope and a sign on the door which read "PRIVATE PARTY." Sam tried the door. It opened easily. She stealthily walked in and all sixteen guests stopped talking and turned to her. A tall, handsome man wearing a lounge jacket and an eyepatch approached her with a bottle of Perrier Jouet. He placed his arm around Sam and turned to face the guests. "Everyone, this is Kudra Oldenfelcher."

The guests approached Sam and greeted her. Some of them were quite put off by her khaki shorts and shirt but they smiled graciously anyway. Sam whispered to the man with his arm around her. "Kudra Oldenfelcher?"

He whispered back. "Gives them something else to focus on rather than who you really are."

"My friends call me Patch. What do your friends call you?"

"Sam. Nice boat."

He turned to Sam. "There is a boat stationed in the aft deck. This is a ship."

"Of course it is."

"*My* ship to be precise and, why am I allowing you to stay on it?"

"Because you were smart enough to get good champagne."

He laughed while reaching for two glasses. "Good answer." Patch poured the drinks. "You know, downstairs, I have a cocktail dress you might feel more comfortable in."

Sam held up her glass to toast. "That might be nice. What else have you got downstairs?"

They both heard explosions and looked towards the forward deck. "I will give you the full tour of the ship but why don't we watch the fireworks first."

Most of the other guests had already headed for the rear upper deck. Sam left her backpack and followed Patch. The fireworks lit up the sky and the reflection in the small, dark, body of water they were in. It was a little chilly and Sam placed her arm next to Patch's arm sleeve. A drunk woman approached her slurring her words. "Hi, I'm Catherine Arly and you're...."

"Kudra."

"Oh yes, Goldenbelcher. You're not related to the New Paris Goldenbelcher's are you?"

"Well, you know what they say 'Ol man Goldenbelcher sure did get around."

Catherine Arly laughed too much at the poor joke. "That's funny. I thought you might be related. How do you two know each other?"

Patch interrupted. "We're cousins. Haven't seen each other in years. And, she certainly has grown."

"Yes," the woman laughed. "In all the right places."

Patch looked at Sam. "Perhaps we should find you some warmer clothing."

"That sounds like a good idea."

"You'll excuse us Miss Arly."

"Oh, you go right ahead. I'm gonna go flirt with the helmsman."

"Don't steer him off course Catherine."

She laughed spilling some of her drink. "Oh, we've done that already."

Catherine exited towards the helm and Patch addressed Sam. "Shall we?"

"Lead the way."

Sam followed Patch two flights down and into a corridor. Everything was white and clean.At the end of the narrow passageway, there was a door labeled 'Captains Quarters.'

Patch unlocked the door. "Make yourself comfortable." Patch went through another door and closed it behind him. He left Sam in a small, dark, wooden room. It had the smell of wood polish and the ever-present scent of the sea. She noticed a cluttered desk and a few chairs in front and back of it and a file cabinet with a few maps hanging out. She sat in the captain's chair and swiveled around to see the fireworks coming out of the brass portholes. Patch re-entered, leaving the door open. "I hope you don't mind but I've decided to make you an official member of the crew."

Patch held his arm out to direct Sam into the room. She got up, walked in and could not help but notice the blue negligee with matching sailor cap lying on a king size bed.

"That doesn't look very warm. I don't see how I'm going to be watching the fireworks with that on."

Patch looked sincere when he spoke, but Sam had her doubts. "Oh, you'd be surprised. Go ahead and put your uniform on. You'll be warm and seeing fireworks in no time."

"I can only imagine" Sam mentioned as she looked over the attire.

"It's a standard issue uniform," added Patch "You can change in my office."

It took Sam only a few minutes to change. The 'uniform' was tight but fit her curves exceedingly well. "Where would be the best location to view the fireworks?" She asked sauntering into the room.

A low whistle came out of Patch's mouth. "On the bed I suspect," replied Patch taking off his jacket.

"I thought that might be the case."

Patch took off his shoes and lay next to Sam. He looked fully into her eyes as if to ask for permission before kissing her fully on the lips. "Are you seeing fireworks yet?"

Sam grinned. "Oh yes, and I'm getting warmer too."

Patch smiled and kissed her again. Outside of the ship there was a much bigger explosion.

Patch looked up. "They always start without me."

Patch started kissing Sam again but was interrupted by another explosion. This time it tore through part of hull and water was coming in.

Patch got up quickly. "Sorry, I wanted you to see the fireworks not experience them. We have to get out of here." Patch handed Sam a life jacket. "Put this on."

"You have a plan?"

"A good captain always does."

Patch opened a wide door. There was a motorized water cycle attached to it. He took it off the wall and started it. "Better hop on. I don't think we're safe here."

Another explosion impacted the ship. This time water came gushing in.

"What about the other guests?" Sam yelled above the carnage.

Patch started the motor. "They'll be ok. Hang on!"

Sam climbed on behind Patch and they sped down a ramp that lowered in front of them. Sam looked back and saw pirates firing pistols at them and other pirates taking the guests of the ship as prisoners. She yelled "I thought the captain was supposed to go down with the ship."

Patch grinned while adjusting his goggles. "You've got it all wrong. It's the captain who goes down on whomever he pleases."

Sam laughed. "Ah, is that why you're saving me?"

An explosion in front of them knocked them off the water cycle. The bike sank while Sam and patch came up for air. They saw the smoking cannon attached to a pirate spaceship hovering in front of them.

The spacecraft sounded like a blender set on liquefy. Patch and Sam could see sparks flashing off the side of the ship. They let their life preservers keep them afloat while they raised their arms in surrender. Patch coughed up a little water and faced Sam. "About that saving you part. I think you may have spoken too soon."

CHAPTER 20

The transport stopped in front of a sign reading Stadium City. In the foreground, a city of dozens of outdoor and enclosed stadiums of various heights and widths could be made out. Some of them were too far away to discern. Inside of the transport were Silvia, Mel and several people all dressed in black sportswear including two of whom were selected to be their escorts. The emblems on all their jerseys read Titans. The transport took them past a few stadiums where the roar of sports fans could be heard. It stopped at an enclosed arena and their wrist-coms admitted them into the stadium then guided them to their court side seats through the loud fanatics. As the crowd sitting around them hurled insults at a referee for making a bad call, Mel waved his hand to a robo-server pitching hot dogs, popcorn and sodas. The All Mites took possession of the ball and dribbled it down court. They had great passing skills and moved the basketball around like it was in a pinball machine. Before twenty-four seconds had run out, the All Mites got the ball to Rondell Phipps, their star player and power forward. He made a move spinning inside the paint and jumped to attempt a left-handed dunk. Unfortunately for him, Marcus Langtree, the all-star defender was too close behind him and swatted the ball almost a half-court away where Deb the Dunkster ran with it unchallenged.

She leapt from the foul line in a 360 spin and slammed the ball for two points with her right hand. The Titan fans went crazy as the Jumbotron replayed Deb's amazing dunk. Mel and Silvia stood with the rest of the fans yelling their approval, but Silvia's yelling soon got mixed up with her giggling when her escort wrapped his tail around her right leg.

CHAPTER 21

Snow-capped mountains loomed six miles beyond the stadiums. There, hundreds of ski bums tried out their skills while further down the slopes, robo-ski instructors gave lessons to visitors who were a little timid about the higher elevation challenges. Inside one of the ski lounges was a fireplace with a long bar. A male bot-tender was attached to a train that had an engine at each end. It would move the bot back and forth along the bar serving drinks supplied by a large tube secured to his back. He took a glass from above his ever-smiling face and poured a beer from the end of openings on his fingers. One of the customers, sitting by the floor to ceiling window and watching the good and not so good skiers, drained her glass of wine and walked up to the bar. She placed her glass on the bar and waited for the bot-tender to accost her.

"Another glass of chardonnay?"

The woman looked at her wrist-com. "Uh, no thanks, I have a date."

"Lucky you."

The woman smiled. "Yes, but would you send a bottle to my room?"

"Of course," the bot replied. "236?"

"Yes," she said walking out of the lounge and zipping up her ski jacket. She took the first robo-driver lined up outside the bar. Their heads and midriff were attached to the two-person vehicle. The vehicle linked with her wrist-com and sped off on its skis to her private cabin. The outside of the cabin looked like a traditional log cabin, but when the door automatically opened, the latest designs for living in convenience shined in stainless steel. She looked towards the kitchen and spoke. "Slow roasted white chicken pieces, cooked in a white wine sauce with bacon, mushrooms and onions and rice on the side. "

The kitchen-bot began taking things out of refrigerator next to it and the cabinets above it while the woman immediately disrobed. She headed for the shower and asked her wrist-com to play Earth, Wind and Fire. After a few moments, she heard a chime and looked at her wrist-com inside of the shower. There was a tall good looking man at her door. She buzzed him in. In exactly three minutes, he was behind her inside the shower.

"About time" she announced after feeling his hands caress her.

He placed his hands on her waist and kissed her on the neck. "Oh yes" she moaned.

He was the same male physimager that was in the hotel with the businessman. The man turned her around and lifted her until she could wrap her legs around his waist. They took their time kissing hard on the lips and then begin the process of making love. She closed her eyes and was very vocal about the lovemaking in the shower. She shook with pleasure and took a deep breath then opened her eyes and peered into his. They were green and glowing. She smiled.

"Hey, what's up with your eyes?" She looked down and discovered that her breasts are blended into his chest. She screamed in terror.

He covered her mouth with his hand and his hand mixed in with the skin on her face.

He smiled. "Shhhhhh."

The physimager expanded, becoming her normal giant slug-like self, breaking apart the glass shower and slowly dissolving the woman inside of herself. The antennae on her head were rotating wildly and she grinned enjoying the consumption of her victim. The physimager returned to her male human form, walking out into the living room area without damaging his feet on the shower glass. He put his clothes on while listening to "You Can't Hide Love," combined with the sound of the shower spraying water onto the floor uncontained. At the bottom of the shower floor, a small piece of the physimager's skin slowly wriggled, lost its glow and became still.

CHAPTER 22

There were not many seagulls or sparrows in the expansive blue sky in the barren area away from the games, rides, sports arenas and shows, but there were plenty of warbirds. Elliot scuttled his camouflaged, tan and green P-40 Warhawk with gleaming teeth under its nose, into an upward climb to target his fifty caliber machine guns at a P-47 Razorback Thunderbolt. Of course, the guns were not real but they made the appropriate rat-ta-tat noise. And the enemy plane, when fired upon, would develop holes and emit smoke before spiraling towards the ground. The classic World War II fighter planes were powered by Cerrium batteries which made their motors relatively noiseless. But the pilots enjoyed a full range of special effect noises generated by the plane's coms.

The P-40 Warhawks were usually operated by a single pilot but Elliot had requested a co-pilot seat for Cindi, a choice she immediately regretted as their plane began an accelerated curve that had them both clinching their teeth. When he had the Razorback in his sights, he fired but passed by the enemy fighter too quickly to elicit any damage.

"I'm going to circle behind em!"

Amid the noise and the centripetal force, Cindi felt she could only get one word out.

"NOOOOO!"

Her protest was unheard or ignored as Elliot maneuvered directly behind the enemy fighter jet. He surrendered controls to the twin machine guns behind him to Cindi hoping she would get more involved.

"FIRE!"

"I can't!"

"FIRE!"

"I CAN'T!!"

A silver P-51 Mustang came along broadside. It had an angry grimace, baring metal teeth in the front. Those teeth opened and bit through Elliot's tail and his Warhawk spun out of control. The seats became capsules that joined. He and Cindi were both ejected out of the plane.

"What happened?" Demanded Elliot as they plummeted towards the ground.

"I couldn't reach the controls!"

"Oh, come on! They were right in front of you!"

Cindi did not answer. They descended several hundred feet before their capsule released a parachute and the couple were caught abruptly updraft in a cross breeze. The panel in front of Elliot read 'CONTINUE or DISENGAGE.' Elliot decided to talk to his co-pilot first.

"I thought you wanted to do this?"

Cindi yelled. "Because you said '*this was going to be fun.*' Well, you have your fun!"

She pushed her DISENGAGE button and her chute gently glided her back to the ground. Elliot pushed ENGAGE and wings and a propeller nose grew out of his capsule. He climbed pursuing the enemy and fired his smaller machine gun to disable a Messerschmitt while laughing. "This is fun!"

CHAPTER 23

The sign to the disco arena read Paradise Lounge. Candra walked in displaying her wrist-com so the fee would be deducted by a big guy dressed in black from head to toe who looked bored out of his wits. Candra could hear the loud music coming from the band and eventually saw the hundreds of people bobbing their heads or jumping to the rhythm as if they were under some spell by the leader of the band. He looked like the ancient Roman emperor Caesar dressed in a white and purple toga with a laurel crown and appeared to be performing perfectly well although there were several daggers sticking out of his back. One of the two statues next to the band came to life and slowly walked out to the dance area. He pointed his sword at some of the audience members and out of curiosity, Candra stopped. She saw a beam of light come out of the sword and drown several people in its light. The people's images were transported to the big screens. They appeared to be out in an open, deserted field and a spacecraft landed nearby. Two short, green aliens with black eyes and over-sized heads walked down the ramp of the ship and fired their laser pistols at them dissolving their flesh while they screamed in agony.

The crowd went into a frenzy and the music continued. Candra shook her head and followed her wrist-coms direction to a more secluded area. After walking down a dark corridor, she came upon another booth with another similarly dressed and similarly bored man. This one happened to have even more mass.

"May I help you?"

Candra looked at him wondering if he could be the same man, just bigger.

"I'm looking for mister Q."

"Two-hundred seventy-five credits."

Candra reluctantly raised her wrist. "Arnie?" After a few attempts, she gave up on Arnie and finished the transaction herself. The man handed her a bag with yellow powder.

"*This* is mister Q?"

"No refunds."

"Why thank you, and what am I supposed to do with this?" She responded sarcastically holding up the bag.

"You can use the room straight ahead to your left. The door will be open for another twenty-five seconds. Better hurry." The big man smiled and Candra looked at him with disdain but scampered down the hallway and closed the door behind her.

"Arnie stop playing games!"

Arnie did not respond and Candra found her way to a bench in the poorly lit room. There was a smoking pipe that looked like a naked woman surrounded by snakes. Candra placed the small bag on the table next to the pipe. A door slid open and a face appeared. He looked middle-aged, had a bald head but a full beard.

"Candra I presume?"

"So, you're mister Q?"

"At my service. You have something for me?

"If the price is right." Candra took off her backpack and slowly took out the Byrinium crystals. They faintly lit the space with rainbow colors.

"I see it pays to visit the Yarr sector on occasion." The man said smiling.

"Does that mean my timing is good?" Candra asked.

"Twenty-eight hundred a gram good."

"Thanks for the offer but I think I'll look around." Candra started to tuck the crystals away.

"Good luck."

"Do I look like I need it?"

"Thirty-two hundred and that's my final offer."

Candra studied mister Q's face for a short while and brought the crystals out again.

"Bullshit but I accept. Transfer the credits to my wrist-com. Arnie?"

"I'm sorry but you'll have to place the merchandise in the compartment to your right. For verification. I'm sure you understand."

A drawer slid open and Candra just looked at it. "I'll put *one* in."

"As you wish."

Candra placed one of the crystals in the drawer and in a few moments could see that several thousand credits were transferred.

"And the rest?" The man asked.

Candra placed the whole bag in the drawer. "Keep the bag."

A few moments later Candra confirmed the rest of the payment.

"You're a wealthy young lady. Congratulations."

"Thanks, but I'm sure you'll do better."

"It's been a measured pleasure." The man started to fade from view.

"Oh, one more thing."

He came back into full view. "Yesssss."

"How do I find Ozoz?"

The man laughed briefly. "You don't find Ozoz darling. If Ozoz wants you, he'll find you."

Candra walked out of the secluded area and through the disco arena to the exit. When she got outside she found a robo-cab and sat in the back seat.

"Destination please."

Candra paused briefly and then spoke. "Ozoz."

To Candra's surprise, the cab took off. "Well Arnie, looks like we're going to see the man. Arnie? Oh, hell with you."

CHAPTER 24

At an outdoor stadium, a rugby ball was kicked high into the air. The receiving team's captain, Rob Knight, dressed in a black shirt and shorts, took the ball and immediately passed it to the player behind him. The insignia on his shirt and the rest of the team read Buccaneers. The opposing team, dressed in blue, called the Orca's, tackled each man as they scurried up the field but were a little late apprehending the actual ball carrier as they easily passed the ball backwards laterally to the next carrier. When the Buccaneers got two-thirds of the way down the field, the ball got tossed to their big man, Bennie Brougham, who ran it in, breaking tackle after tackle. The big man dived pass the goal line with three men still on him. The Buccaneer fans in the massive stadium erupted and were gyrating like they were little kids being treated to ice cream on a hot day. Mel and Silvia were seated in private boxes cheering, drinking and doing the ritualistic celebratory dance with their new escorts.

In a bedroom where the game was being played on a TV wall, Cindi was packing her clothes. Elliot, by the bedroom door, watched her impatiently.

"Do you have to do this now?"

"Why, is there a better time Elliot?"

"Look, I'm sorry! I promise it won't happen again. I promise."

Cindi stopped packing. "Your promises don't mean squat. Before we left, you said it would *never* happen. I should have known better. I shouldn't have come here." She resumed packing.

"Cindi, I thought we were a team,...I tho...."

"Look, I did not come here to be your fricking teammate OK? You should have invited one of your boys if that's what you wanted."

"Cindi, it's you that I want. Let's just calm down here. Okay, okay, you can choose the rides, games, whatever. I'll go along with it. Whatever you want."

"I want to leave Elliot. That's what I want. I'm done with this."

"You mean you're done with me?"

"Yes Elliot, done with this, with you. Everything. Ok?"

"But we just got married Cindi."

"Oh, come on. It was only a two week wedding pass. We lasted a week. Big deal."

"It was a big deal to me."

"Yeah, well, better luck next time. I'll see you around.

Cindi used her wrist-com to tell her luggage to follow her. The door closed after she left and Elliot sat on the bed watching the end of the rugby game. He switched to an ice skating championship, grabbed a bag of popcorn and started eating it slowly as tears streamed down his face.

In a larger bedroom, the ice skating championship was playing on the wall opposite to the head of the bed. No one was watching. There were twice as many colored bottles of various types of liquor lying about as there were people. Buccaneer sports clothing was strewn all over the floor. Mel disentangled himself from a few people on his bed and got up. He put on a robe and sauntered wearily into the kitchen passing a couple leaning against each other in a forgotten slow dance. He got a glass of cold water and turned to the table where Silvia was sitting watching the ice skaters. He lifted his glass of water to her and she returned the toast.

CHAPTER 25

The hooded guide never said a word to Candra. He used his arm to indicate which way she should go and when she reached her destination, an indeterminate white room, he disappeared. Candra did not know which way to turn to address the being she was supposedly working for, so she just looked up. "Mister Ozoz?"

She looked at her wrist-com but knew it would be useless to get help from Arnie. He was in a bad mood. "Damn useless program" she muttered. Behind her, the whiteness was replaced by what could only be described as a section of space. She was mesmerized by the scope of the portal and the magnificence of the stars before her. At the same time, she was frightened. The voice came from all around her.

"I trust you have received your credits."

"Uh, yes. So you're,..."

"I am Ozoz."

"What are you?

"A vital part of this planet and in some respects, the guardian."

"So, you're like,...... God?"

"Everyone is like God."

"Yeah but, people are afraid of you."

"But not you?"

"Well yeah, you're a pretty scary cat alright. No doubt about that, but listen, I'm not really good at playing detective. I don't know where you got your information but...."

"You are correct. You are not good at playing detective nor being one. That is not why you are here. Your job is to keep agent Bicks from harm. He will bring the creature to me. You will prevent it from destroying him."

"Creature?"

"The Physimager."

"Ah ha. And what happens if this creature destroys me?"

"You have unique survival skills. *That* is why you are here."

"I see. You got this pretty much all figured out. So, you take care of this here planet as well as the inhabitants cause from what I understand, you've gotten rid of some folks yourself."

"What I did was to protect the innocent."

A small section of space spiraled with dark clouds and then became a portal looking back at a primitive time on the planet. People who looked like the ancient Maya of Earth but wore long robes with hoods to avoid the sun, carried a man bound at the wrists and ankles and threw him into a deep crater with lava flowing at the bottom. Ozoz explained.

"The fairer-skinned ancestors of this planet knew of me and would sacrifice their own in an attempt to please me."

"Why did they do that?"

"Fear often motivates erroneous decisions."

"So, you made yourself known to them."

"The ones who were doing the sacrificing got to know me. For a brief while."

"I bet you surprised the hell out of em."

"The sacrifices ended."

"Until now?"

"You are referring to yourself. There is a small chance you will not survive the encounter with the shape shifter. However, you may decline now without reimbursement."

"Sounds tempting but I think I'll take my chances."

"As will I."

"Humph, you don't seem like the kind who takes a lot of chances."

"Otherwise you would not work for me."

"Now ain't that the truth. So how do I find this... agent Bicks?"

"You will recognize him easily. My guide will escort you out."

"And the rest of the payment?"

"It will be transferred to your ship when the job is complete."

Candra turned and the small, hooded man was there waiting for her. "Okay Ozoz, see you around."

Ozoz did not answer. The view of outer space closed and the white room became seamless again. Candra walked in the direction the now present hooded figure pointed towards until she was outside in the dark tunnels with the same cab waiting for her. She climbed into it.

"Police headquarters." The cab sped off and Candra spoke softly out loud. "One of the more interesting characters we've ever worked for Arnie." Arnie did not respond.

CHAPTER 26

The early morning light reflected off the glass windows of the tall buildings where many of Maze's guests resided. Several-hundred feet below, Elliot walked in the shadows of the buildings towards the amusement park area. In solitude, he walked past empty rides; The Hurricane, Rhonda's Rumpus and many other rides that were closed. The loud screams that normally accompanied them were a faint memory. Eventually, he got to the end of the park where he knew one amusement would be open. It was only a two-story antiquated house that looked gray in the bright morning light but it was actually painted black. The sign on the door read: "Domicile of Death". Underneath in smaller letters it said, "Always Open."

Elliot opened the door which made the obligatory creaking sound. He thought the smell of rot alone would keep people away but forged ahead and saw cobwebs everywhere covering ancient hand-held weapons and monitors of people being executed from years past. There were more than a dozen doors inside that looked like they had not been opened in years. Eventually, his eyes came to rest on a still and incredibly old, pale black man with a white beard.

The man was mostly hidden behind a dusty booth and wore a black hooded robe. He looked at Elliot and spoke like he was too tired to do so.

"May I help you?"

Elliot was reluctant but decided to go ahead with what he had planned. "I want to die."

"Of course you do. Please,... have a seat."

Elliot saw a dirty bench to the left of the man. He wondered about the last time someone had come to this 'amusement'. He sat down and the man spoke again looking somewhat concerned. "Now tell me, why do you want to die?"

Elliot had trouble getting the words out. "My wife,.... my wife left me."

"Oh, yes. That is terribly unfortunate and, a very noble reason for termination. Is there a particular way in which you would like to end this terrible circumstance you have been dealt?"

"No, it doesn't matter."

"Ah, I see. Why don't you step this way."

Elliot got up and followed the elderly man to one of the black doors. He opened it and there was a large wheel with a needle pointing at zero. The small picture behind the needle indicated that someone had frozen to death. Around the circumference of the wheel were more than a dozen ways for someone to die.

"This is the Wheel of Death. I am sure something suitable will turn up. Heh heh."

The man's laugh at the pun sounded more like he was coughing. He stepped out of the way and Elliot took hold of the wheel. He gave it a spin, feeling its weight and watched it slowly turn. The needle came to rest on number twenty-three and there was a sword behind it.

"Ah" the old man uttered with a slight smile on his face. "One of my favorites. If you will just transfer fifteen-hundred credits, I will make all of the necessary arrangements."

Elliot spoke to his wrist-com. "Transfer fifteen hundred to the...."

"Domicile of Death."

"Domicile of Death."

A screen rose in the old man's booth. It was the only thing that looked somewhat new and clean. The old pale man looked at it and then returned his attention to Elliot. "Very good sir. Now if you will kindly step this way into the Booth of Finality."

Elliot walked over to another door and the old man opened it. "When the curtain opens, you will have thirty seconds to walk out. If you do not walk out in the allotted time, the termination process will be cancelled but there will be no reimbursement. Do you understand?"

Elliot swallowed. "Yes."

"Do you have any last words sir?"

"No.... yes. Tell Cindi,... tell her that I love her."

"Very good sir. Have a glorious death."

The old man closed the door and Elliot found himself in a small closet without light. Moments later, a curtain opened. There was a loud roar from a lot of people as Elliot made his way out into the bright sunlight. He shielded his eyes and after a few seconds, he could make out an enormous coliseum filled with a multitude of yelling people. It was an ancient Roman scene and he was in an arena. The crowd filling out the circular stadium were all wearing garments of the era. The emperor rose from his seat and the noise subsided. He extended his arm and gave the thumbs down signal and the crowd went wild again. The emperor was the same lead singer at the Paradise Lounge without the knives protruding out of his back.

The arena crowd became more exuberant as a gladiator walked out from a sublevel in the structure. He was a large man with short hair but bushy sideburns. Battle worn with scars on his bare chest to prove it, he raised his sword and helmet high into the air with a big grin and the noise from the masses was deafening. He slipped the helmet on. It was silver and had two long extensions that looked like fangs. He turned to Elliot, who now looked as though he would rather be back in the Booth of Finality and as Elliot looked out at the crowd, the gladiator plunged his sword deep into his chest. Elliot made a sputtering sound and fell onto the hard, dirt ground. He felt numb, his vision blurred but when it cleared, he saw two glowing women with halos hovering above him. They flew down to him, their wings stirring the dirt up as the gladiator and the rest of the spectators seemed to not notice, instead, they kept cheering at Elliot's demise and the person waving his arms who caused it. The angels lifted Elliot upwards and before he flew out of the stadium, he saw a young lady resembling Cindi who appeared to notice his ascent.

Somehow, he heard her say above the mayhem, "I love you Elliot."

Elliot felt relief. He smiled as the two angels took him to a dense area of clouds. They smiled and gently dropped him off on solid footing although he could not see his feet nor his surroundings as he strolled through the mist. He saw some light up ahead and made out a gate.

It was made from wood, painted white and had a sign above it which read: "Welcome to the other side." Elliot walked past the gate. He felt no pain and the wound in his chest had magically healed. As he walked further, he could hear the faint noises of people having fun. The clouds cleared. The amusement park was open and Elliot was back at the entrance to The Domicile of Death. There was a sad young man about to enter.

Elliot accosted him. "Your first time?"

"Nope, twelfth."

Elliot smiled and walked towards "Rhonda's Rumpus".

CHAPTER 27

The outside of the pirate ship looked like a silver barrel with short black wings protruding out on either side. It had chrome plating and the six black cannons sticking out of brass portholes looked like truncated legs. In the front midsection of the ship, the pirate emblem was prominently displayed. Above that and behind a glass panel was a sophisticated com panel where the captain and his first mate toasted with rum poured from a wooden cask. Inside the ship and two decks below, the interior was not so pristine. The walls and floors were made of old wood planks and everything was wet and musty.

Sam and Patch were waiting in line with the other captives in vine handcuffs. They heard a woman scream from outside the ship and both looked towards the exit. Once outside they realized the reason for the screams. They were both sprayed with water to clean them for a potential buyer. There were several small pirate ships out on the water. The captains were on board looking over the captives and one particularly foppish captain in bright colors and a tall hat selected Sam and Patch. The pirates spoke gibberish but seemed to comprehend each other. Sam could not help but start giggling.

Patch looked at her with a wry smile on his face. "What's so funny?"

"Oh, I think I had too much grog last night."

"Oh, right."

"You know, I must say, I am quite disappointed I didn't get to perform any of my duties as your First Mate."

"Ha, what was last night?"

"Ohhh, so those were the kind of duties you had in mind?"

"Yes, and I must say, you performed your duties with exceptional skill."

Sam laughed out loud until a gruff looking man in his late thirties approached them with an extremely serious look on his face. He was excessively hairy but bald on top, wore only leather straps and metal rings and brandished his antiquated pistol to guide Patch and Sam down a ramp onto a small boat. After they were situated, the scantily clad man aimed his pistol at the side of the boat. The pistol emitted a sound that caused the boat to grow vines that attached to Sam and Patch's vine handcuffs. He also shot near Sam and Patch and the boat grew eyes to watch the captives.

"Are we supposed to act afraid?" asked Sam, who started giggling again.

"I think we are. Shall I ask mister charismatic?"

"Please don't."

The water was calm and clear as the captain boarded the vessel. The boat was decorated like him; colorful and ostentatious. He was helped onto the boat by a grumpy looking fellow and then sat in a comfortable lounge chair. He discharged his gun at the side of the ship and it grew oars that started rowing downstream. His servant gave him something to drink and fired his pistol once more at the vessel and it grew a waving fan for the captain. Sam started smiling at the captain in a flirtatious manner. "I wonder if he's willing to share what's he's drinking?"

"No harm in trying" reflected Patch.

Sam's smile did not go unnoticed. The captain smiled back at her and told his hairy helper in their language to provide her and Patch something to drink. The servant maintained his unpleasant expression while pouring the prisoners drinks from a canteen. He then brought two wooden mugs over to Sam and Patch and lost the unpleasant expression on his face by pouring the drinks over their heads. The captain started giggling and it developed into a full blown cackle.

Sam looked at the laughing captain. "Must be pirate humor."

Patch was distracted by something else. From a distance, he could see several fins making their way towards the boat. "Looks like we have company."

Sam looked in the direction of the fins. "I hope this grog acts as a shark repellant."

"I don't think they're interested in you."

As the sharks got closer, the captain shot the sides of his boat again. More oars grew out of the side and the vessel gained speed to counter the approaching sharks. He yelled something to his assistant indicating that the sharks were gaining on them. The grumpy fella procured a bat and prepared to club the approaching water adversaries.

When the sharks started circling the boat, the unpleasant fellow started swatting them with his bat but one of the sharks grabbed it away with his teeth. He yelled and shot at the boat and it stopped rowing and began hitting the sharks with the many oars. The sharks not only ate the oars but began eating the boat as well. The boat grew several mouths, began screaming and disengaged the vines attached to Sam and Patch's wrists and ankles. When the captain realized it was a losing battle, he shot at his fan and it became a propeller and flew him in his seat above the mayhem. The grumpy fellow continued to fight the sharks even though there was nothing much left of the boat. Sam and Patch swam away. Not too far from them was an island where they swam ashore exhausted. Breathing heavily, Sam lay on the beach and started laughing again.

"I think I'm beginning to like sharks."

The couple heard some drumming in the background. They sat up and turned to see the natives of the island approach them. They held spears and had no heads on top of their shoulders. Their smiling faces were in the middle of their chests. Sam lay back down and laughed harder than she could ever remember laughing.

CHAPTER 28

Agent Bicks stared out of the living room window of the cabin. He watched with an ever so slight smile at the thing he had always wanted to try, skiing. And even though it was a man-made mountain with man-made snow and the skiers were wearing t-shirts in the fair weather, the thought still enticed him. Felker and Wex, perused the cabin and were followed by the maintenance worker who let them in. He looked like a ski bum with long dreads.

"Come on man. Why don't you just level with me? It was the Ozoz that got her, right? Isn't that what's going on here?" Felker was more than annoyed. "No."

"Aww come on man. Why else would you guys be here?"

Felker walked into the bathroom to look at the broken shower again. The water had been turned off. The maintenance man followed and stood at the bathroom door. He used his thumb to indicate Bicks and asked Felker. "Isn't that dude G.B.I.? What's he doing here?"

"Look Tweedle dee, like I said earlier, we just want to look around. If we find out anything, you'll be the last to know, I promise you. We can let ourselves out so why don't you go chase some snow bunnies or something."

Felker walked out of the bathroom as Bicks walked in. He could hear Felker arguing with the maintenance man in the living room area and then what seemed to be a struggle. Amongst all of the broken glass, he thought he saw something moving. On closer inspection it looked like a sliver of glass but it appeared to have minute legs. He used another piece of glass to pick it up and placed it in a plastic bag then put it in his coat pocket. Bicks walked out of the bathroom.

The maintenance man was handcuffed in a chair with duct tape over his mouth. He tried to complain to Bicks but Bicks just addressed Felker. "Let's go over to the lab."

"You got something?"

"Maybe."

Bicks, Felker and Wex exited the cabin. The maintenance man yelled after them as best he could and after a few moments, Felker came back.

"Now," he said taking a pause. "You gonna behave yourself?"

The maintenance man nodded with enthusiasm.

Felker patted him on the back. "That's a good boy."

Felker then took a ski cap from a coat rack and after fitting it snugly on the maintenance man's head, walked out again smiling. The maintenance man was hopping mad.

CHAPTER 29

From outside of Lillie's bedroom door, her parents were eavesdropping. They could hear Lillie talking. "No Sharon, you have to share your biscuit with Abigail. It's only fair. What do you say Abigail?" Janice knocked on the door before opening it. Inside, Lillie was seated around a small table with a life-size doll and five small dolls. One of the small dolls spoke. "Thank you." They all turned their attention to Janice and Richard Feucks.

"Hi Mom."

"Hi sweetie. Your father and I are leaving now. If there's anything you need, ask Clara. Okay?

"Yes Mom.

"Goodnight Lillie, see you in the morning. How's the tea?"

Lillie and all the dolls responded with a smile and all spoke at once. "Gooood."

Her parents smiled as well and closed her door. Their smiles slowly dissipated as they approached Bradley's door and heard the usual loud sound of war games. Roland knocked.

"Yes?"

He tried the door but it was locked. "Your Mother and I are leaving. Can we talk to you for a moment?"

They heard the sigh come through the door. "All right."

Bradley opened the door and stepped through to avoid his parents from seeing too much inside. Roland continued. "You haven't finished your program yet?"

"No, not yet. Almost."

"Well, finish it soon. We're leaving and you need to help take care of Lillie. We talked about this."

"Yeah."

Janice interrupted. "We also talked about your room Bradley. We're not going to pay an extra cleaning fee just because you can't keep your room tidy. Do you understand?"

"Yes, I'll clean it. Promise."

"Alright son, have a good night and don't stay up too late."

"Yes, sir. Good night Mom. Have a good time."

"Good night Bradley."

Bradley closed his door. Inside, there were food wrappers, male and female toy warriors, blankets, toy guns and various war games strewn everywhere. On his walls were the usual scenes of space and ground warfare. The heavy metal bands were gone. Bradley picked up a remote and pointed it at a life size doll seated across from him.

The life size doll was dressed in an Eagle Scout's outfit and stood up when Bradley pushed the 'engage program' button on the remote. "Hi, my name is Andy. Let's find something fun to do."

Bradley walked over to the toy boy and punched it hard in the stomach. The toy bent over as if it were in pain. "Oaaaff!"

Bradley smiled. "I already have. Now bend over and lick my shoe, barf slime!"

The boy toy, already bent over from the hit to the abdomen, kneeled and started licking Bradley's shoe.

Near the exit door, Janice was addressing the maid, Clara. "I don't think you'll need to check up on them much but if there's too much noise coming from Bradley's room, don't hesitate to let him know."

Clara smiled broadly. "I'm sure he'll be fine."

Roland reached into his jacket pocket. "We're going to pay you in advance. I assume credit vouchers are ok?"

"That'll be just fine." Clara stuffed the vouchers into her apron. "Have a wonderful time at the Palisades."

Roland opened the door. "We're certainly gonna try."

Janice closed the door. "Thanks Clara, see you later."

Clara took the vouchers out of her apron, counted them and stuffed them back in.

CHAPTER 30

Candra got out of the auto-cab and looked at the building that was police headquarters. It was night and looking at the dark gray stone building she was reminded of old detective movies she had seen in her Lillum tank. The difference was, it did not fit in with the modern buildings around it. She walked up to the door opened it and saw an auto-cop behind a glass partition.

"So much for antiquity" she murmured.

The auto-cop addressed her. "May I help you?"

"Yes" Candra replied, "I am looking for a detective."

"Any particular flavor?" The auto-cop said without changing his dull expression.

"Flavor?"

"Robbery, homicide, kidnappi....."

"Yes, that's it."

"Homicide. I suspected as much. I will need to see some ID."

"Oh, well, my wrist-com is on the blink. Uh…. Arnie? I don't know what's wrong with it."

"Did you report your wrist-com malfunction?"

"No, I just got here."

"You will need to go to the visitors center and get a working wrist-com. Otherwise, I cannot help you."

Candra shouted at her wrist. "ARNIE!" She then took a milder approach with the auto-cop.

"Look, I don't really need a detective. I'm looking for a G.B.I. agent, Bicks. We're supposed to be working on a case together. If any of your people know of his whereabouts, can you please let me know?

The auto-cop was silent for a moment. "We all know of his whereabouts" .

Three more partitions slid down around Candra. She was trapped in a thick, plastic cubicle.

From the ceiling, automatic weapons with scanners descended.

A loud recording broadcasted. "Do not move! You are being scanned for weapons and determination of species."

Candra pounded on the clear wall. "Oh come on!"

Captain Mozilli walked towards the auto cop and could hear Candra yell at him over speakers.

"You wanna let me out of here? What the hell is this?"

Mozilli spoke quietly to the auto cop. "Good looking out Ben. Did the dead wrist-com tip you off?"

"Not as much as her desire to see agent Bicks. Must have a thing for GBI. No weapons."

Mozilli watched the monitoring screen while listening to Candra's protests. "Definitely human."

"More than."

"How's that?"

Ben pointed out Candra's bio chart. "Can't be too sure without cutting her open but everything looks a little too good."

Mozilli watched Candra through the glass. "I'll say. But Ozoz mentioned something about protection. I guess she's it. Raise the panels."

"Be careful."

The panels slid upwards and the guns receded. Mozilli walked towards Candra but kept his distance. "Good evening ma'am. I'm Captain Mozilli. And you are?"

"What the hell is the meaning of this! I didn't travel across a hundred parsecs of space to be treated like some common criminal!"

"The physimager is no common criminal, I assure you."

"I ain't no freaking physmager, or whatever the hell you call it!"

Mozilli walked closer to Candra. "No, you are not. Perhaps you'd like to step into my office."

Mozilli stepped to one side and Candra walked through the precinct glaring at everyone.

When they got to Mozilli's office, he sat down and offered Candra a seat opposite him. She sat. Mozilli took a Tylenol lolly out of his desk and offered one to Candra.

Candra spoke slowly and deliberately. "No thanks."

"So, what do people call you?"

"Candra."

"That's it?"

"That's it."

"Ok Candra, at risk, I'm going to assume you are Agent Bick's protection?"

"That's what Ozoz says."

"You've spoken to him?"

Candra relaxed. "Yes."

"And you think Ozoz is looking out for us poor little human folk."

Candra smiled. "Maybe he's bored."

Mozilli returned the smile. "That I would understand. But I doubt it."

"Actually, I think he cares about us. He's likened himself to a caretaker."

"He also said he was an amusement."

"Who's he amusing?"

"Himself? Perhaps it's just one big four dimensional game we're in but not aware of."

Candra sat back in her chair. "Yeah well, he plays on a very broad game board."

"And so he does. What are you going to do about your wrist-com?"

"Can you get me a temp?"

Arnie suddenly came back to life. "You wouldn't dare!"

Candra looked at her wrist. "Watch me while you still can."

The wrist-com on Mozilli became active. It was Ben the auto-cop. "Captain, there is a problem at the Hyatt/Hilton."

"What do you mean by problem?"

"They think it's another disappearance. A businessman from the Harston-Olvac conference."

"Get me a copter and muster all of the mini-copters you can within a ten mile circumference of the area." He looked at Candra. "Also, inform agent Bicks of the situation. Ready to earn your keep Candra?"

"I was born ready."

Arnie popped back onto Candra's wrist-com. "I knew you were kidding."

"Don't push it Arnie."

CHAPTER 31

Upon entering the Grand Pavilion showroom, one might think they were entering the Emerald City of Oz. Everything was green, glittery and there was the strange canned, familiar, theme music with voices singing praises as if you had already won big at the main attraction there; Kash Kart Karavan. Mel and Silvia followed the other contestants being led by a tall, attractive woman in a short, sparkling green dress and matching hair. She did not talk to them, just smiled her green lips broadly and gently placed green Mardi Gras type necklaces over their necks with a large number attached to it.

The contestants were ushered into a waiting area behind a rail with large, spinning, gold dollar signs on it. There were screens to look up at that had 'Kash Kart Karavan' flashing in and out in bold green letters. A curtain behind the railing opened to fanfare as twin doors opened and the contestants flooded into a room where there were mobile carts. When all the contestants had settled into their individual carts, the stage curtain opened and the applause sign inside, lit up. An unseen announcer welcomed their host, Glenn Gelswang and he strutted into thunderous applause, some by the contestants, some pre-recorded. Before the applause died down, Glenn Gelswang spoke in a voice amplified by a hidden mic on his suit.

"Welcome to Kash Kart Karavan. Let's see who our lucky contestants will be today as I spin the Winsome Wheel!"

As Glenn spun the Winsome Wheel, all twenty-four mini-carts with green headlights, automatically rotated their passengers in a quick spinning pattern on the floor. The audience members seated upstairs cheered the contestants on. When the needle settled on number thirty-one, Mel's cart moved to the front of the line and he was called up to the stage. One could hear Silvia scream with delight throughout the entire showroom. Mel felt like screaming as well but mostly out of fright. He had heard that Gelswang's head was bigger in real life but did not appreciate the actual enormity of it until now.

Apart from the sparkling silver color, Gelswang looked like an outlandish version of the Wizard of Oz replete with large lapels and a tall hat that only added to the largeness of his head. Moving uncomfortably close to Mel, he asked for his name inches away from both of their heads. Mel responded but kept his eyes on the host's grin which seemed to have more teeth than the standard human mouth. Hearing Silvia scream at him convinced Mel to turn out to the audience, smile and pretend he was not nervous. "And where are you from Mel Raspalo?" The game show host inquired.

"New Indiana." Mel replied, hoping that would be the end of the interview. "All right!" said Gelswang turning out to the audience. "You can take your chances on the Big Wheel or.... I can offer you one-thousand credits right now. Oooooor, you can take your chances with the Krazy Kart Klowns."

On cue two clowns came out and danced around Mel. They were short, like midgets, had the typical clown costumes but their heads displaying maniacal grins were almost as large as Gelswang's. Mel paused while almost everyone yelled for him to go on to the Big Wheel of Winnings. In the history of the game, no one had ever taken the money instead of going on to the Big Wheel of Winnings. A few decided to go with the Krazy Klowns. Most of the time, the Klowns would play a bad joke on you but on rare occasions, you could win big with the Klowns. He looked at Silvia seated in her cart towards the back and could read her lips.

"Big Wheel!" He said to Gelswang.

"Alllllllright! Oooooooon to the Big Wheel of Winnings you go!"

Mel got back into his Kash Kart and it attached itself to a Ferris wheel. Glenn Gelswang announced the other five riders who came after Mel and the Krazy Kart Klowns danced around them as well. They all decided to go on the Big Wheel of Deals. Gelswang pushed a button in the middle of the Winsome Wheel while broadcasting loudly, "heeeeeeeere we go!"

The button set off a ringing noise and then calliope music started as the Ferris wheel slowly turned the contestants around in its circular path. The twenty-four contestants in the carts and the audience upstairs worked themselves into a frenzy. As the Big Wheel of Winnings slowly came to a stop, the noise from the contestants came to a crescendo.

There were six indicators in the center of the Big Wheel of Winnings, two allowed riders to stay on, one gave a rider five-thousand credits, one turned the cart over to the Krazy Kart Klowns and Mel got the one choice left that bumped him from the ride and the show. The Klowns danced around in dismay because no one was picked for their amusement. Glenn Gelswang patted Mel on the back. "I'm sorry Mel from New Indiana. Try us again another day on the Karavan of Kash Karts. I'm going to spin the Winsome Wheel to see who's next on the Big Wheel of Winnings and who of our upper section will be joining the 'Karavan of Kash Karts!'"

A beautiful model escorted Mel to the backstage area. He was given a basket of treats and coupons for other rides and discounts to other shows. He thought about hanging around to see how Silvia would do but decided to go back to their flat and play with his favorite escort Baba until Silvia returned. "Or long after she returns" he thought smiling.

CHAPTER 32

Clara walked down the hallway humming and carrying a tray with a tall glass of lemonade and a plate with cheese and crackers. She knocked on Bradley's door a few times before he responded behind the closed door. "Not now!" Clara unlocked the door and walked in. The room as well as the toy boy were totally trashed.

"What are you doing? You can't come in here without my permission!"

Clara smiled. "You haven't been very tidy".

Upon noticing Clara, the toy boy greeted her trying to raise his broken arm and its voice was damaged as well. "Hi, my name is Andy. Would you like to pla...."

"Shut up and heal yourself."

The toy boy began to repair itself and Bradley pointed towards the door. "You need to leave now."

Clara looked for a place to set down the tray and then offered the drink to Bradley. "I thought you might like some nice cold lemonade."

"Nice cold lemonade? What are you nuts? Is that why you're still working here? Somebody felt sorry for you? You should have been replaced by a bot ages ago. Have you considered retirement?"

"No, not really."

"Well, you should! Now would you please get out of here and take that crap with you and don't come back into my room unless I ask you to. Are we clear?"

"Perfectly, however, there is one thing I would like to show you."

"Make it quick."

"As you wish."

The maid changed into her natural physimager self. The green glow from her body could be seen on Bradley's face as he exclaimed. "Whoa!"

The front door connected to Janice Feuck's wrist-com and opened to their apartment. Once the encrypted password was accepted, the door always said "Welcome." Janice however, was not in such an accepting mood. "That is not what I am saying. What I'm saying is to not have Owen book *anything* for us again."

Roland knew coming home way before they had intended was mostly his fault but tried to deflect. "Honey, we went over this. How could Owen possibly know Tarr Ventures was not going to be there?"

"Well, he has a history of screwing things up and mostly for us."

"Yes, alright, but he did book us for tomorrow night, right? Tarr Ventures et al. What is the big deal?"

A scream was heard, and Janice turned her attention down the hallway. "Bradley!"

Both parents ran down the hall. Bradley's door opened and Clara was there.

"Where's Bradley?" Janice asked. "What happened?"

"I don't know." Clara answered. "I heard this scream and came running but the boy's not here."

Roland shook his head. "I've completely had it with him. If he thinks he can leave whenever he...."

Roland was interrupted by Janice's scream. He looked where she was looking and in the mirror behind Clara, saw the lower part of Bradley's leg and his shoe protruding out of Clara's back. Clara smiled. "I guess you'll be wanting your vouchers back."

Roland started at Clara with incredulity. "WHAT KIND OF A MONSTER ARE YOU?"

He picked up a cluttered chair and tried to smash it across Clara's head but Clara just grabbed it from him and crumpled it. Her eyes started turning bright green and Roland decided that running from Clara was in their best interest. He and Janice sprinted down the hallway yelling out to Lillie. Before the three of them got to the door, the physimager in her natural giant, slug-like form, came crashing through Bradley's bedroom wall. Roland frantically tried to make an emergency call on his wrist-com while the large doll from Lillie's room came out. She started to speak but the physimager swallowed it into itself and immediately spit it back out. This gave Roland enough time to get what was left of his family out of the apartment.

CHAPTER 33

Sam and Patch were captives again. This time by primitives whose faces were a part of their torso. Their new captor's language was even stranger than the pirates. It included winking, whistling, humming as well as speaking babble. They all wore grass skirts, were barefoot and adorned themselves with many leather and wooden bracelets around their ankles and wrists. The females were distinguished by breasts where eyebrows would normally be and they would raise a breast when intrigued. There were two small flaps on top of their shoulders covered by hair that suggested ears.

The captives were led in leather manacles to the middle of a camp where happily excited natives rushed out of their tents to see the newcomers whose heads atop their shoulders amused them to a stance of pointing and laughing. They took turns hand feeding Sam and Patch food and drink just to see how they utilized their mouths and necks and were mesmerized watching them.

Between sips and bites, Sam thought the whole experience was amusing and laughed out loud which garnered even more interest from the natives. Even when Sam and Patch talked to each other, it seemed to amuse the natives.

"Looks like we're tonight's entertainment" mentioned Sam.

"And tonight's meal as well." Patch responded motioning towards the large pot sitting on the fireplace. Sam looked at the large black pot and a woman placing vegetables and spices inside of it. "Oh, come on! I thought they only did this in antiquated movies and bad ones at that."

"Well, you have to admit this is sort of like a bad movie."

Sam laughed out loud again and Patch leaned in and kissed her. The natives responded with "Oooo's" and "Ahhs" and then stood them up and walked them over to the large pot.

A thick wooden ladder was placed against the pot so the captives could walk into the pot. Sam looked back at Patch. "Isn't this the part where we get rescued by the cavalry?"

Patch's eyebrows creased. "Don't tell me you haven't been in hot water before?"

"Very funny mister."

Sam walked up the ladder and jumped into the pot. "Hey, it's not bad. Like being in a hot tub."

"Exactly" Patch replied.

"Are you trying to tell me you've done all this before?"

Patch jumped in beside her. "Well, I haven't done you before."

"Quite the flatterer, aren't you?"

"You wouldn't want me to lie would you?"

"Yes, as a matter of fact, I would."

"Well, in that case...."

"Shut up and kiss me."

With his hands still tied behind his back, Patch pressed himself against Sam and slowly kissed her on the mouth. The natives giggled and suddenly there was a terrific explosion coming from the nearby formally declared dormant volcano. They both looked towards the heavenly spew. The natives ran about hysterically gathering things and running away from the camp. In very little time, Sam and Patch were alone in the camp. The liquid made it easier for Patch to slip out of the manacles and he untied Sam's binds.

"Shall we make a run for it?" Sam asked.

"There's time." Patch replied as he embraced Sam and kissed her again. Their kiss was interrupted by the volcano erupting again.

CHAPTER 34

The crime lab was a large white room with a computer that took up the entire side of one wall. Bicks looked like a small toy figure in the middle of the room sitting in a lone chair. He took a sip of coffee before deciding to begin.

"Computer"

"Authorization code required."

"Bicks, 7241 sec com 29."

"Access granted."

Bicks removed the tissue sample from the clear plastic bag from the inside of his coat pocket and placed it on a glass surface. "Display tissue analysis."

The computer made a soft whirling noise and a read-out displayed itself on a screen above the tissue. Bicks read it quickly, silently moving his lips. "Introduce colbalt infusion with same analysis." Moments later another read-out was on display.

"Uh huh" Bicks muttered. "Does analysis of tissue determine physical capability of shape-shifting?"

"Insufficient data."

"I thought you might say that. Can analyzed tissue be recognized by remote scan regardless of shift?"

"Affirmative, on level seven diagnostic scan."

"Load all mini-copters in section J with level seven diagnostic scan and scan for determined tissue entity. Also, load tracking info on P.E.T. disc. Display tracking and scan results here and patch into Captain Mozilli and detectives Felker and Wex."

"Engaged."

The computer's screen divided itself into sections revealing Captain Mozilli riding in a copter with Candra. It also displayed Felker and Wex in a police transport and the crime scene at the Grand Hilton where police were talking to the Feucks family. Janice Feucks was seated and hugging her daughter, Lillie. Roland was talking to the officers. Bicks studied the scenes carefully and linked various people's wrist-coms to evaluate what was transpiring. It was obvious the perpetrator had attacked the Feucks family as well as the businessman at the same hotel. Bicks conveyed the information to the detectives, Mozilli, and chairman Mekkel's office.

Philimus Mekkel was staring at the same divided screen in his office. He looked closely at the Feucks family studying their distraught faces and read their testimony about the attack that took their son from them. He watched captain Mozilli and an extremely attractive woman in a chain mail dress disembark from a copter and approach the uniformed police. Bicks came up on his screen suddenly.

"Chairman, the mini copters remote scans have identified the perp. He is heading west on Mulgarden just past Dixon Place. The detectives are enroute."

Mekkel leaned back in his chair. "Thanks for the update Agent Bicks." He turned his chair around and faced Kelde, standing and sipping his favorite medication. "Perhaps we can get this wrapped up soon."

Kelde raised an eyebrow and took another sip. A smile slowly formed on his face. Mekkel wondered if it was the news or the drink that caused Kelde to smile. He knew better than to ask. Bicks popped out of view on Mekkel's screen and he looked at the figure the remote scans were identifying as the physimager. At the top of the screen, it read 'Entity of tissue origin targeted."

The figure was that of businessman Fred Chalmers from the Harston-Olvac merger. He had been missing for several days and presumed dead. Now he was walking in broad daylight down Mulgarden street, but the scans had linked his skin to the sample Bicks had taken from the shower where another victim had disappeared. Suddenly Chalmer's was looking directly at Bicks. Somehow, he must have noticed the silent mini copters. Chalmer's ducked into a local pub and Bicks reached out to the detectives. "Identity of physimager confirmed. Disguised as missing businessman Fred Chalmers. Current location, Ryan's pub, 1625 Mulgarden street. I will meet you there."

Bicks picked up a small black suitcase which read P.E.T.A. on the side of it. Underneath, it spelled out 'Programmable Electronic Tracking Apparatus.' "Computer, terminate session." The computer screen faded to black and Bicks rushed out of the room.

CHAPTER 35

Glen Gelswang took Sylvia by the hand and helped her out of her cart. She was at least twenty years older than the popular TV host but hoped he would notice her flirtatious smile and her matching silver outfit with the silver sparkles in her hair and of course, the low cut top with ample cleavage spilling out. She even wore silver lipstick. Unfortunately, he did not seem to notice any of it. His attention was entirely turned out to the audience.

"And your name is....."

Silvia turned out to the cheering audience as well. "Sylvia Saunders."

"And where are you from Syyyyyyyllllllvia Saunders?"

"New Indiana."

"Our second guest from the auspicious colony of New Indiana. So Sylvia Saunders, how about one-thousand credits to give up your turn on the Big Wheel of Winnings or a chance with the Krazy Kart Klowns or do you want to move on to the Big Wheel?"

The audience was yelling senselessly again for Sylvia to go on to the Big Wheel. She pretended to be indecisive and then blurted out "The Big Wheel!"

"Alright, but wait, wait, just one second, since you came all the way from New Indiana, I'd like to offer you a special deal. How about two-thousand credits to give up your chance on the Big Wheel? I have it right here."

Glen Gelswang pulled an envelope from his silver jacket and counted out two-thousand credits. Sylvia smiled while the audience became more boisterous. She shook her head. Glen took more money out. "Three-thousand credits, final offer."

This time, most of the audience turned their concerns towards Sylvia to take the credits. Sylvia looked at the stack of bills smiled and shook her head again and once again repeated "Big Wheel." Glen Gelswang raised his arm and pointed to the Big Wheel. "On to the Big Wheel of Winnings you go, Sylvia Saunders of Neeeeeeeeeeew Indiana!"

Sylvia got into her cart and it joined the other carts on the Big Wheel. Glen pushed the middle button on the Big Wheel of Winnings. The calliope music started again and the carts spun around while the audience cheered them on. The Big Wheel slowed and eventually came to rest. Two contestants got to stay on, one got a five-thousand credit voucher, one got bumped from the show and Sylvia's needle pointed to the position she dreaded. She would be rendered to the mercy of the Krazy Klowns.

After she was helped out of her cart, the Krazy Klowns danced around her to their own drunken carnival music and Glen Gelswang greeted a new Klown dressed in a tuxedo who handed him a letter. His features were out of proportion as was his walk.

"Well Sylvia" Glen started, "the Krazy Kart Klowns have offered you an invitation to a race! You can accept the invitation ooooooooor, you can get inside of this barrel!"

Another Klown came on dressed in protective gear from head to toe. The upright barrel he rolled out on wheels had an oversized lock on it, was full of water and something in the water was furiously trying to get out. It was an easy decision for Sylvia. She chose to race. The barrel was carted off and the Big Wheel glided away from view. A Klown came on with a tall cowboy hat and a pistol and gave them to Sylvia. She put on the hat and while another Klown rode out on an inflatable rubber duck. The duck was big enough for Sylvia to get on and practice bouncing up and down. Another Klown came out in complete cowboy attire riding a bouncing duck and got close to Sylvia while giving her dirty looks. Glen got between them.

"Ok, ladies and gentlemen, the race is about to begin. Our contestant Sylvia Saunders, will be riding against Wild Bill Biggles to the finish line. There may be a few distractions but that's never stopped our contestants before, right audience members?"

The audience members shouted in unison "NO!!"

"Then let the race begin!"

Glen Gelswang was handed an oversized pink gun. He aimed it high into the air and shot off a subtle bang with lots of sparkles and confetti. Wild Bill set off quickly but almost immediately fell off his duck. Four more Klowns came bouncing out in native African costumes and circled Sylvia and Wild Bill clobbering them with large balloons and reciting some war cry.

Wild Bill used his pistol to shoot at the balloons and when they popped, the Indian holding them would ride away. Sylvia did the same. The audience members cheered on Sylvia between laughs.

Sylvia took a slower pace but was moving well towards the finish line. This went on for about five minutes with Wild Bill passing Sylvia but then falling off his duck until Sylvia crossed the finish line first. Wild Bill finally dragged his duck across the finish line and walked off stage obviously disappointed. Glen walked up to Sylvia. "Our winner is Sylvia Saunders from Neeeeeeewwww Indiana. Congratulations!" The Klown in the tuxedo awkwardly walked up to Sylvia and shook her hand vigorously. His fake arm fell off in the process. Sylvia screamed and the audience laughed. "And now, Sylvia Saunders, because you are the winner in the Krazy Klown race, you have the opportunity to choose your prize." A curtain opened and three doors were revealed in separate pastel colors and covered with sparkles.

"You can choose door number one, door number two or door number three. Now mind you, there is a prize of fifteen-thousand credits behind one of those doors so pick carefully. So what will it be Sylvia, door number one, door number two or.... door number three?"

Sylvia paused for a moment while the audience yelled their choice for her. Glen leaned in close to her face and she spoke. "Door number three."

"All right, audience members, Sylvia has made her choice. Go ahead and open the door you have selected, door number three."

Sylvia walked up to the light blue door and opened it. Immediately, a giant hand with a cream pie almost as large slammed into Sylvia. She was covered in cream pie from the knees up. The audience went wild with laughter and the Klowns danced around Sylvia.

"Well," Glen said smiling, "looks like you picked the wrooooong door Sylvia. Our hostess will help you with the clean-up and we will move on to the next contestants for the Big Wheel of Winnings!"

CHAPTER 36

The copter slowly descended onto the roof of the Hyatt/Hilton's heliport. After Mozilli clambered out, he watched Candra exit more gracefully. They walked away from the copter while a uniformed cop yelled above the noise.

"If you follow me, I'll take you to our provisional HQ."

The four mini-copters hovered almost noiselessly above the passenger copter and remained there while the larger copter powered down. Mozilli and Candra followed the cop into an elevator and down to the lobby where the Feucks family could barely be seen behind the heavily armed police. Candra looked at the chandeliers and the fancy wallpaper thinking this was going to be a vastly different kind of gathering the lobby was generally used for.

Janice and Lillie Feucks were crying and embracing each other. Roland was seated. His hands covered his downcast face. Mozilli looked over the family and turned to the lead cop. "Get these people outta here. Take them to a secure location." He walked over to Roland. "I'm Captain Mozilli. I am deeply sorry this horrible thing has happened to your family. We are close to apprehending this... thing. Carson will take you and your family to a secure location and we will keep you updated as we make progress. Again, I'm terribly sorry."Roland stood up. His eyes were red and full of tears. "What is that thing?"

"Other than being a shape-shifter, we're not sure sir. But we will stop it. That I can promise you. Please go with Sargent Carson. He and his men will escort you to a safe location. Carson."

"Yes captain?"

"Send those mini-copters over to where Felker and Wex are going."

"Yes sir."

Roland Feucks slowly gathered his family and they left with three armed policemen towards the roof where a passenger copter awaited them. Candra finished looking over the report.

"Shall we go back to our copter captain?"

"By all means." Mozilli noticed Candra appeared preoccupied "Anything in that report I don't already know?"

Candra had trouble getting the words out. "It was a boy, eleven years old. Only his right shoe remained."

Mozilli attempted to maintain a professional image but the regret in his voice was obvious as he headed up the stairs. "Yeah."

———

The pubs on Mulgarden all had different Irish names but resembled old-fashioned small, dark, pubs right down to the smell. Even the robo-tenders along the long row of bars all had thick Irish accents.

Robert Chalmers walked leisurely down Mulgarden Street. He had a lot to drink, for a human. Practicing the human form with a slight swagger, he comfortably greeted strangers while looking for a new victim in an uncrowded bar. Noticing a mini-copter discreetly trying to follow him made him choose the closest, Ryan's pub. The robo-tender looked similar to all the other robo-tenders on this street; balding, gray with a decent beer belly and always smiling. This one was chatting up two red-faced men seated at the other end of the bar but didn't keep Chalmers waiting long.

"Hello laddie. What can I do you out of?"

Chalmers knew what he would have without looking at the extensive beer list. "A pint of Kinnagan's Red." He had already sampled four of them at other pubs and liked the taste.

"There ya go son." The barkeep dropped off the beer and went back to his prior conversation. He was interrupted again as two more men burst into the bar. One had a gun drawn and the other a high-powered rifle. Both were aimed at Chalmers. Chalmers took a sip of his beverage and slowly spun around in his stool to see Felker and Wex standing near the entrance. Felker was looking at his wristcom to verify Chalmers identity. Wex, holding the rifle, looked more nervous than usual. Chalmers smiled at the detectives and then diverted his attention to the bartender. "These lads will have the same as me barkeep."

"Belay that." Felker blurted out. "We're here on business."

The place was as still as the grim expression on Wex's face. The two men near the robo-tender paid their bill quickly and left. Chalmers did not seem to be worried. "You have no idea what you're missing. This is the best beer I've ever tasted. Of course, I'm not used to ingesting beer."

"Yes," responded Felker, "that's along the line of what we're here to talk about."

Before he disappeared into the back area, the robo-tender pressed a button and the front doors swung shut. A sign appeared on the door saying 'closed.' Chalmers took another sip.

"Oh, I don't think you want to talk. Your nervous friend certainly doesn't. I think you want to arrest me, kill me perhaps, or at the very least, get me the hell off this planet. Isn't that a more likely scenario?"

Felker swallowed. "Probably.........yes."

Chalmers smiled. "Well, that certainly is understandable, I'm probably wreaking havoc with the tourist industry."

"Actually, business has picked up. People have a morbid fascination for these kinds of things."

"Now isn't that the truth" Chalmers agreed nodding. "One of the more fascinating things about your kind. I mean, mixing fantasy with reality. You're bound to get yourself into trouble. Don't you think?"

Felker sighed. "Still....."

"Yes, yes, I suppose you're right. Better to go out gracefully. Besides, with all those copters out there, you've probably got a whole battalion of uniformed police surrounding the area."

"Probably."

Chalmers downed the last of the brew. "Great stuff, this beer. Alright gentlemen, my hands are yours."

Chalmers stood and held out his hands. Felker cautiously placed handcuffs around his wrists. He looked up into the eyes of Chalmers and saw them glowing green. He whipped out his gun and managed to fire once but it was too late. One of Chalmers hands turned into a thick snake and bit Felker a few times drawing blood. Felker screamed. Wex fired bullets and then hot metal rods into Chalmers from his automatic rifle. Chalmers screamed from the searing agony of the rods but then turned his other hand into a snake as well. Both men cried out in pain as they were lifted above the bar room floor by the snakes now entwining and crushing their bodies and then thrown through the large glass window displaying the 'Ryan's Pub' sign in gold, antique letters. Two mini-copters fired gas grenades through the broken window before flying in while two uniformed police recovered Felker and Wex. Several other police in heavy gear, rushed into the pub wearing gas masks and shouldering laser rifles. They only found the robo-server in the back who smiled when they found him. "Happy hour laddies. Two for one."

CHAPTER 37

Cindi looked closely into the hand mirror one last time. Her third eye was bigger than her two normal eyes but the makeup artist was right to be pleased after she finished working on Cindi. She had applied red eyeshadow that complimented the orange and green eyeshadow on her other two eyes and her light-blue, feathered, ear wings. The processional music started. It was Israel Kamakawiwo'ole singing his classic version of 'Somewhere Over the Rainbow.' He did not have the traditional implanted third eye like everyone else at the Vroog wedding because he said that would make it harder for him to play his guitar, but he did have winged feathered ears and wore the Multoonga worm dress.

Cindi's escort, her father, was waiting for her by the door of the dressing room. When she walked out and took his arm, everyone in the over-sized white tent, opened and closed their mouths in an exaggerated manner rapidly and without making a sound. Cindi's husband to be was more eager and faster at performing the mouth ritual than the guests. It was a perfect start for a Vroog wedding.

The long but thin white worm moved around in lavender Rukee water in the priest's dress like everyone else's water dress, but the priest also had a water turban with a smaller worm inside of it. He spoke in English but slurred his words with elongated vowels. Everyone in the audience softly chanted "Zah! Zah! Zah! Zah!" all the while he was speaking. When he finished, he shrieked and the newly married couple turned out to the audience. The chanting got louder and louder until the married couples water dresses broke and the two worms joined each other.

Of course, the Multoonga worms would die once out of the water, but it meant giving life to the newly married couple. There was a tremendous cheer from the invited guests, and before walking down the hall with her Multoonga worm attached to her husband's, Cindi looked into his eyes and experienced the hypnotic effect all the Lillum tank Vroog grooms have. She studied his smooth, strong jaw and the warm, inviting smile. His perfect face reminded her of the other grooms she had married over the last two days. She looked up and said "cease program." Everything disappeared and when Cindi stepped out of the Lillum tank, she was wearing her blue jeans and torn, pink, t-shirt. The Lillum tank attendant approached her.

"You didn't like the Vroog wedding either?"

Cindi looked over to the wedding Lillum tanks she had tried, the Hindu, the royal English and a same sex wedding. "No, it was fun but,…. I just don't think it's for me."

The attendant looked perplexed. "You didn't experience the best part, the honeymoon, on any of the weddings you were in."

"Yeah, I know. I just got out of a marriage. It was only a two week wedding pass that lasted one, but Elliot was a real jerk."

"Ahh, I see. Well, you're young. You should give it some time. Maybe after a few years."

"Yeah, maybe."

"Come back and see us again. We'll have some exciting new programs."

"I will, thanks."

Cindi walked out of the Lillum Tank Wedding Chapel towards the Movieland building. There was a line to get in and an attendant handing out a list of all the movies she could be in as the star, or just playing a bit part. She remembered years ago, seeing movies on large screens. People still did that, but it was a lot more fun to be in one, go to the red carpet world premiere and the wonderful after-parties.

There was the choice of being in a new, original film or be in a re-make. The re-makes had a chance of better reviews and she wondered if she had the right aptitude for Eartha Kitt's role in "The Mark of the Hawk". Cindi knew she would get help from a famous legendary acting coach brought back to life through robo-technology. She also knew the sound technicians would modify her voice to sound like the movie icon but still wasn't sure she could pull it off.

After she came out of wardrobe in a stunning silk robe, she sat in a chair with her name on the back of it and met the man playing the role of Sidney Poitier. She tried not to stare at him but could not help herself. She wanted to say 'cease program' out loud but knew it would not do any good. She was lost in his smile and eyes like a single drop of rain in a thunderstorm. She would work with this man, be his leading lady, get to know him, pretend she was not interested and eventually convince him to go back to the Lillum tank marriage chapel with her even if he was just a robo-actor.

CHAPTER 38

Agent Bicks arrived at 1625 Mulgarden Street just as the robo-medics were loading Felker and Wex into an emergency transport. They were in no condition to speak but the uniformed cops had told him that no one of interest, particularly the shape-shifter, was inside of Ryan's pub. The robo-tender was being downloaded although his recorded information was deficient since he had locked himself into a private room when most of the action started. Bicks did however, listen to the recorded sound a few times to hear the physimager talk to the two detectives before hurling them through the storefront window.

Bicks walked in with the black P.E.T.A. briefcase and looked around. The smell of the noxin gas was still there but he did not need a gasmask. He noticed the three beer mugs and picked up one of them from the bar to smell the leftover brew and then walked to the back area. The small room where the robo-tender had locked himself in was stacked with many boxes of Irish whiskey, coasters, napkins and an opened box of chips in small bags. The bathroom had its own unique smell. It needed cleaning. He also noticed a small drain on the floor that was not seated properly and decided to lift it up to inspect but the sound of his name being called stopped him. He walked out and looked at a thick man and a tall, beautiful woman staring at him with wide eyes. She blurted out "BYRYN!"

He raised his eyebrows. "It's actually Brian, miss, Brian Bicks."

Mozilli raised his hand. "Nice to know you're not just an image on my wrist-com Agent Bicks."

Bicks took his hand and they shook. "Nice to meet you captain."

"This is Candra. I guess you two will be working together on this case. Especially now since you won't be getting much help from my detectives."

"Sorry captain." He looked at Candra. "What is it?"

"Oh nothing." Candra replied. "Ozoz has quite the sense of humor, that's all."

"I'll let you fill me in on that later. I believe I know where our shape shifter has disappeared to."

Bicks picked up his briefcase and led Mozilli and Candra to the bathroom in the back. He kneeled, set his briefcase on the floor and opened it. Inside was an immobile black cat. Bicks took the cat out of the briefcase and pushed a button above its tail. The robot creature elongated, thinned out and grew fins. After sliding open the grate, Bicks lowered the cat into the hole in the floor and the three of them watched it fade away into the darkness.

Bicks stood up. "I encoded the PETA with the shaped-shifters biometric signature. It may take a while but it will find the creature no matter what shape she assumes. I'm linked in via wrist-com and have taken the liberty of patching you in captain. All we can do now is go home and wait."

Mozilli turned to leave. "I'm going to the hospital to see about my boys." He turned back.

"Might be a good time for you two to get acquainted but you may want to go to another pub."

Mozilli did not expect a response. He walked out of the pub not looking back and with a painful smile on his face, realizing it was up to Bicks and this strange woman Candra to solve this case just as Ozoz had arraigned it. He thought perhaps Ozoz should replace him as captain and laughed out loud at the thought of that mysterious creature wearing a badge. A few had talked to Ozoz, but no one had ever actually seen him. Maybe it was better that way.

"If I ever do meet him," Mozilli mused, "I'll offer him the job."

CHAPTER 39

He swung slowly. Imagined himself swinging faster for this drive but there was really no need. The gravity was merely one-third of what it was planet-side and besides, the space suit he was in made it difficult to do anything with alacrity. Nevertheless, the ball traveled past the floating asteroid which was the green, into the ring of this moon they were playing on. Elliot could see the other players shake their heads behind their helmets. He would go two strokes over par and that was not a good feeling going into the sixth hole. The robo-caddie sped ahead with the clubs to where the golf ball had settled in the ring. It was similar to the one on Saturn but was small enough to play the eighteen holes leisurely in half a day. The ring was made out of clear filaments imbedded on a hard green surface and was hard to chip a golf ball out of.

Elliot judged the distance from the flagstaff and hoped it would only be a double bogey. He started walking and partially floated in the low gravity in long slow strides. He could feel himself sweating inside of the suit and needed to go to the bathroom and spoke to the suit.

"Auto-sanitation."

"OHHH!" "Yeow!" "Need some privacy buddie boy?"

Elliot forgot to silence his com-link and he could hear the other three players laugh while his suit took care of business. "Real funny guys." He was glad the other guys could not see the redness he felt growing on his face. Elliot hated golf. He thought playing it in 'outer space' would be fun but now realized he should have played this game at the bottom of the ocean like he wanted to. The suits and buoyancy were about the same but at least he would be able to see a few whales go by. Nevertheless, he would get through this. And when he was done with this game and these guys, he would climb out of this large Lillum tank and find Cindi. Above all else, that is what he really wanted to do.

CHAPTER 40

The snakes that had grown out of the physimager arms and had bitten Felker and Wex while squeezing them to the point of asphyxiation and then hurled them through plate glass, was now one singular snake. Its green eyes glowed in the dark sewage water as it swam near the top to avoid sludge. When the pipe widened and became an upwardly tiered sludge removal system, it knew it had come to the first step of a sewage treatment plant. The overflow from rainwater was released into the warm ocean nearby after filtration. The physimager grew legs and widened its tail to become a fin and swam over to the ocean water.

It now resembled a large salamander with a bald semi-human head. Its four antennae emerged from the side of its face as it advanced towards shore. The creature noticed a school of giant manta nearby and it attached itself to one, at first by holding on to it and then gradually fusing itself to the Manta so that its body now had the large triangular pectoral fins. As it got closer to a swimming area where humans were bathing and frolicking under the blue sun, it once again took on the appearance of the red-headed human woman but walked out of the water without clothing and its side fins were large and fluctuating. A girl approached the creature pointing out the fins and the physimager smiled and let the child rub her smooth black fins. A shrill scream from the child's mother stopped the encounter.

"RUTHIE!!"

Ruthie knew she had done something wrong but was not quite sure what that was. She walked over to her mother who looked very frightened and picked her up hurriedly carrying her away. The physimager watched them for a while and then turned her fins into arms so she looked like a normal human again. She heard Calypso music coming from a resort and started walking in that direction. After a few moments, a long and slender black cat came up out of the water and stealthily followed her.

CHAPTER 41

Agent Bicks was smelling beer again. He had already drank three different ales and decided to try the stout. He nodded in approval and took a few hearty gulps. "Ooh, this is nice. You should try it." Candra looked over the six empty mugs in front of them at the bar and shook her head.

"I think I've had enough for now."

"Mmmm, maybe you're right. We need to get to our accommodations and it has been a long day. Joe, what's the hint of flavor I'm tasting in this stout?"

Joe, the robo-tender at McAlary's Pub, smiled as he poured another customer a beer at the other end of the counter. "Chocolate with a suggestion of cardamom." he said in a predictable Irish accent.

Candra picked up the mug. "You didn't tell it me was chocolate." She downed most of the pint without hesitation. "You're right, it is nice."

"Was nice." Bicks said burping.

"What's that?"

"Nothing, we should go. I'll take care of the bill."

"Allow me. I just sold some... property."

Bicks raised what was left of the mug of stout to her. "Well good on ya. Did you sell a time share here on Maze or maybe I shouldn't ask?"

"Maybe you shouldn't ask." piped in Arnie on Candra's wrist-com, now appearing as a uniformed policeman with an Irish accent.

"Oh god!" Said Candra getting up off the bar stool.

"What is that?" Asked Bicks staring at her wrist-com.

"My own little personal hell, agent Bicks. Joe, transfer the bill to my wrist-com."

"Will do, you kids come back and see us again."

Candra and agent Bicks walked out of the bar and climbed into a taxi. "Aren't you staying at the Grand Hyatt/Hilton?" She asked.

"That's where my luggage is checked in. What about you?"

"I'm staying at the Ozoz inn."

"Really?"

"Yep."

"Well I'll be. How are the accommodations there?"

"I don't know. Last time I was there, there was just a large white room. Couldn't even make out the walls."

"Yeah" Bicks said, "that's what I remember. Didn't know he had accommodations as well. Wonder what kind of breakfast he serves."

"You'll find out soon enough agent...."

"Brian"

"Brian. You're to bring the physimager to him, there."

"Yeah, that is my understanding. I hope he has a decent ale. I might need it."

Candra laughed. "You've come a long way to do Ozoz's bidding."

"Yep, I guess we both have. Why did you say he had a sense of humor? Does he have a night club with comedians there as well?"

"No, not that I'm aware of. It's just that... well, my ships program partner looks just like you."

"Ships program partner, is that like a spouse program?"

"No, just something I do for entertainment."

"Humph, I'll be damned! Cloned without benefits."

"Don't worry, I'll erase the program when I get back to my ship."

"Oh, I'm not worried. Actually, I think you should keep the program. After all, there's a good chance I may not come back in one piece after visiting our physimager friend."

"Is that your vain attempt at immortality?"

It was Brian's turn to laugh. "Yeah well, maybe. Don't we all want to be remembered?"

"I'm sure you have loved ones that will remember you agen.....Brian."

"GBI agents don't have time for romance or family. We're on assignment throughout the galaxy so we're given program-mates."

Candra frowned. "Program-mates, doesn't sound very romantic."

"Yeah, but if one of our agents has a fixation on a certain program-mate, he, or she, can secure that program and marry it."

"And how many program-mates have you married?"

"None."

"Why not? I'm sure there's no alimony."

Brian chuckled slightly. "No, no alimony. Guess I'm holding out for the real thing."

"Think you'll be able to tell the difference?"

"Yeah, the program–mates are better lovers, better cooks, they only talk about things you want to talk about and, you can turn them off whenever you want without any complaints."

"And the problem is…….."

"Well, they only do what they're programmed to. Humans, on the other hand, have the gift of unpredictability."

"That's a good thing?"

"Sometimes. I mean, sure, you can program the program-mates for unpredictable behavior or whatever, but it's still something you or someone else programmed. Besides, wouldn't it bother you to know that your true love only exists in a Lillum tank?" Candra did not answer for a while. She stared out of the taxi window and spoke. "Maybe when they perfect androids, it'll be different."

Bicks scoffed. "Ha! Those companies all went out of business. It's never worked. Lillum tanks are cheaper and, you can change your partner at the drop of a hat,… so to speak."

There was another pause before Bicks spoke again. "How long have you been with yours?"

"My what?"

"Your program-mate."

"Long enough. Arnie, delete the Byryn program."

Arnie had the same face, but his eyes were popping in and out. "WHAT?"

"You heard me."

"Are you sure abou...."

"Arnie!"

Bicks looked like he was falling asleep, but he opened his eyes. "Your com has a mind of its own."

"To say the least."

As they passed by the Palladium Stadium. Bicks almost silently let out a whistle noticing at least fifteen twenty-something ridiculously beautiful women waiting in line to get in. He wanted the taxi to slow down so he would have a better chance to scrutinize each one, but of course, it picked up speed. As a consolation, Bicks decided to study the woman he had avoided studying because he was trying to be professional.

Later on he thought he would blame it on the ales. Candra had a body that was even too good for a goddess. But Bicks was subtle about staring at her. That is, until he discovered that the occasional light passing through her chain-mail dress revealed she was wearing no underwear. The taxi slowed down and announced Bicks destination. "Grand Hilton." Bicks pressed the LED exit button on the display and the door slid open. Before leaving he looked back at Candra.

"I know you're supposed to be my protection but are you going to be okay alone with Ozoz?"

Candra stared at Bicks briefly. "Are you trying to invite me up to your place, Agent Bicks?"

"Just looking out for my partner."

"Yeah, you've been looking alright."

"That obvious, eh?"

Candra leaned towards Bicks until her lips were almost on his. "You should quit while you're behind." She kissed him fully on the lips as he sunk back into the seat. "Not bad for a human. Let's see what else you can do."

CHAPTER 42

Even with a steady intake of oxygen, Felker had trouble breathing. Of course, his three broken ribs did not help in that regard. Sleeping was even more troublesome. He tossed and turned in the hospital bed trying to get comfortable and only when he was too tired from a lack of sleep and had enough drugs in his system did he manage to do so. Still, he woke up to the sound of an IV dripping, a few robo-nurses wheeling around the hallway and the electronic machines monitoring his current health state. He hated hospitals. He felt too tired to open his eyes and too affected by the drugs. His throat was dry and he decided to reach for a glass of water next to his bedside. Felker opened his eyes and turned his head to see where the glass of water was. He tried to move his arm to pick it up but could not manage. Somehow, both of his arms were immobilized.

Even though it hurt him, he leaned forward and saw the problem. Both of his arms were attached to the female version of the physim-ager. Blended together. His torso was also attached. They were joined at the waist and arms. She raised her head and Felker could see her antennae move around on her head. Her breasts jiggled as she started to laugh out loud. Felker's eyes widened as tears slid down them and although he was wearing a breathing apparatus and it hurt him to do so, he managed to scream out loud. The scream woke him up. There was no physimager he was attached to. A robo-nurse wheeled in smiling in that hideous fake human way robo-nurses smiled. "Are you alright here?" She asked, readying her four arms to administer meds or whatever was required. Felker turned away from her. "Just leave me alone."

The robo-nurse checked his vitals and wheeled out of his private room. Felker closed his eyes again but the tears continued.

CHAPTER 43

At the foot of the bed, Brian Bicks dark blue suit lay on the floor next to Candra's chain-mail dress. There were other minor clothing items scattered about the large, dark room but what disturbed Brian was the one black sock he was sporting on his right foot. He stared at Candra suspecting she was awake but appeared to be sleeping and decided to get up and make coffee. Perhaps that would make her happy he thought. It would definitely make his head happy. Those ale's he consumed last night had more kick to them than he had bargained for.

Brian slipped on his briefs and after a futile search of ten minutes, gave up on finding the other sock. He loosely put on his shark-skin purple shirt and walked into the kitchen. There was a voice controlled coffee machine which made him smile. He whispered 'two lattes' and studied the layout of the space. It was a small, luxury suite with a sauna and a deck overlooking most of Maze. Apparently, Maze/Cor wanted him to feel more than content with his accommodations and he appreciated the gesture. He heard a chime coming from the kitchen and went in to get the lattes. Candra remained motionless in bed. Maybe, he thought, she was waiting for him to leave. He placed her latte on a nightstand next to her and drank his, got dressed and quietly left the apartment. On the rotating ramp leading to the elevator, he thought more about his night with his 'protector.' They both were a little too careful with each other knowing they both had not been sexually involved with a real human in years. It would take some getting used to. He could feel her stare and turned towards the suite while waiting for the lift. She was standing at the window, her nudity partially hidden behind a sheer curtain and partially behind his missing sock she was holding. For a moment, he thought about going back, but the elevator door slid open and he backed in slowly almost cracking a smile.

CHAPTER 44

They saw the fountain on the outside of the isolated building. It was a quiet area, away from the crowds and the noise. The white porcelain fountain had the same glitter and brightness as the building and it released a fine mist that gave the appearance of a holographic rainbow. Above it, a sign read 'The Fountain of Unlimited Possibilities.' Mel and Silvia stood there staring at the centerpiece as if they were indecisive about going into the building, despite the fact that they had already paid an exorbitant price for this venture.

The hesitation was more about what they would have to go through. There was no limit as to how much time they could spend there. It would all depend on how much they could endure the strain of the tubes and electrodes feeding and draining their bodies while the Lillum tank simulated real-life dream states for them. They would become super athletic twenty-five year old's and their minds would have genius level capabilities.

"Are you ready Mel?" Silvia spoke with a slight hint of trepidation. Mel nodded. "Of course."They walked in holding hands, fondly remembering the reason for this costly trip to Maze, their thirtieth wedding anniversary. The double doors swung open and there were three attractive people there to greet them. They all looked to be human. The male of the trio encoded their wrist-coms after their identities were verified. "Mel Raspalo and Silvia Saunders, welcome to The Fountain. Are you ready for a fabulous and life altering adventure?" Mel and Silvia looked at each other and said "yes" simultaneously. The male host smiled and nodded.

"Well, if you follow your escorts into the prep room, they will get you ready for your transformation."

The tall women, one black haired and the other blue, led them through another set of double doors into a large room that had gold paneling with white walls and a gold and glass chandelier. There were two doors at the other side of the room with Mel and Silvia's name embossed on them. The black haired woman spoke. "Please disrobe and put on the suits provided for you in your changing room. The program choices are on the wall panel. Take the time you need to choose your careers. We will close up the uniform heads for you and please don't forget to wear your slippers."

"Well I guess this is it." Mel said with an impish smile.

Silvia laughed. "See you soon handsome."

After Silvia closed the door of her changing room, she examined the attire she was to wear. The gold jumpsuit was obviously made to custom fit her. It had silver lines running through it and tubes protruding out of the nose, mouth and genital areas. The slippers were plain and black. She looked at the long list of career choices and gently pressed a few areas on the touch screen. Silvia took off her jeans, shirt and underwear and put on her jumpsuit. It was cold to the touch and felt like a light, wet suit. She stepped out of the dressing room and walked over to the women.

"I see my husband is taking his sweet time."

"You were very quick at making your career choices." The blunette replied.

"Cause I knew what I wanted before I got here."

Several minutes later, Mel came stumbling out of his dressing room and was surprised to see Silvia waiting. She laughed. "Looks like you're going for a swim on Pluto."

"I had a tough time choosing." He responded.

The escorts took the couple by the hand and the four of them walked into another room. Inside were Lillum tanks for Silvia and Mel. Other than the normal monitors, these Lillum tanks were equipped with tubes and wires that would be connected to the suits. There were also very large helmets with all sorts of tubes.

"Are you ready?" The blunette asked.

Silvia said yes and Mel nodded. "See you in a few days." He said and then kissed his wife.

The women took off their slippers and closed up the head pieces on each suit. Silvia and Mel could not see as they were guided into the Lillum tanks but felt the helmets being strapped on. In the darkness, a soft humming noise was heard and then there was light as Mel was helped out by the blunette. He covered his genitals with his hands and did not understand why he was naked, then realized his real body was still in the Lillum tank.

There was a full-length mirror nearby and he could not help but look at himself. He did not look any different. He was still bald on top and had the same midriff bulge. He had a double chin and there was little muscle tone to see. He was not fond of his body at sixty-one, and before he could walk away disappointed from what he saw in the mirror, the blunette handed him a gold chalice with the initials FUP engraved on them.

"Drink all of it." She insisted.

Mel slowly poured the drink down his throat. It was thick and was unusually pleasing to the taste. He tried handing the chalice back to his helper, but she was gone. He then felt his head itch and started to scratch it. But looking into the mirror, he noticed that his hair was starting to grow back. Mel started laughing and began to notice that his protruding belly was receding. The soreness in his hip was gone and he was starting to lose the bags under his eyes. "Whoa!" he yelled emphatically. In a matter of minutes, he had returned to the age of twenty-five. Mel was so gleeful about his new look and feel, he was bouncing around until he realized that activity was uncomfortable with an erection. He stopped, looked again in the mirror and felt the solidness of his young body with his hand. He then decided it might be a good idea to find some clothes. There was a closet nearby and Mel opened it. Inside was a baseball uniform and Mel could see 'Raspalo' written on the back of it. He took the uniform out of the closet and turned to see the other players getting dressed in the locker room.

The noise from the sold out stadium was deafening. The Boston Badgers had swept the New Tokyo Tigers in four games and now, it was the first game of the World Series. After Roger (Beanball) Benson struck out the first two batters, Mel stepped up to the plate. He remembered what it was like to play college hardball years ago and if he could now live up to doing what the coach, his teammates and the yelling fans apparently thought he could do. However, the pitcher for the Badgers was not taking any chances. He casually threw outside of Mel's hitting range, forcing Mel to walk. At first base, Mel studied the pitching style of the star pitcher and knew at some point he would steal second base. He got his chance when the catcher dropped the ball on a fast, errant pitch. Mel was amazed at his own speed. He knew he could run even faster but had to gauge his slide into second. He was safe. He spit out some of the dirt that was all over his St. Petersburg Pirates uniform and sported a big grin at how easy it seemed to steal a base. The pitcher threw the ball with more regularity at second base to keep Mel from considering another steal but his teammate, Bobby Hoskins, hit a sacrifice fly knowing Mel could outrun the outfielder after he caught the fly ball.

He did and the Pirates were up, one to nothing. The game ended that way and the Pirates celebrated with champagne in the locker room. All of his teammates congratulated Mel and they all agreed that they would do much better in two days without the Badgers ace pitcher, Orson 'Beanball' Benson on the mound. They also all agreed to go to Sally's and the bat boy told Mel that he would pull his Lamborghini out front for him. Mel found a sharkskin green suit in his locker and put it on. He let the bat boy drive them to the bar and grill, where Sally had a vodka tonic waiting for him. There was also a sports reporter waiting for him who after getting a small crowd away from him, sat on his lap and whispered into his ear. "I'd like a private interview." She had a Caribbean accent, long dark hair and was stunning to look at. Mel whispered back. "Before or after morning coffee?

"Let's play it by ear," she whispered and then slowly licked the ear she had spoken into.

The next morning, they sat out on Mel's spacious, wooden deck wearing white robes and watched the waves softly splash up on the shore. Mel sipped his coffee and sampled the croissants with strawberries and cream the robo-cook had brought out for them.

"Not hungry?' Mel asked the reporter.

"Not for this." She replied with a wicked smile.

Mel stared at her for a brief while remembering the incredible night he had had with her.

"Yes" he said, gradually returning the smile. "Let's have that interview tonight over dinner."

Two hours later, Mel was dressed in casual slacks and a sport shirt. He watched the reporter sleeping on his bed and then walked into the living area. On his seven foot projection screen, they were replaying his scored run with the Pirates. He opened the front door and found himself looking at a lab coat. Mel put on the coat and heard voices and a TV announcer behind him. He was now in a hangar with two mechanical engineers and two aerospace engineers. They were watching the same replay and noticing him, turned around to applaud and congratulate the star outfielder.

"When did you get back?" Asked Paul Werson, the prominent scientist who had developed a successful one-man air and water cycle.

"Just now." Mel said, not knowing what else to say.

Winston Amberpomba took off his glasses. "It's getting late, I think we better get started."

"Yes" Julia Carter agreed, "I've been staring at your ship all morning."

The five scientists walked over to Mel's small spacecraft. It looked like a typical silver flying saucer but had vents all around the circular underbody. It was a small prototype, only six-feet wide and looked like a toy. Mel had assured them that a larger scale model would not only carry passengers, it would create its own gravitational field for interstellar flight. Mel took the remote and pressed a button. The almost silent turbines lifted the craft off the floor. This was expected. He watched the other scientists anticipating their next reaction and pressed another button. The vessel radiated barely noticeable waves on one side of it and moved in that direction.

Mel had the craft move in any direction the gravitronic waves emitted as he controlled it to on his remote. The four scientists watched with their mouths wide open in astonishment.

"That is amazing!" Grover Jones, one of the aerospace engineers exclaimed. "How did…"

Mel had the craft settle down for a landing. "Let's go inside and I'll explain it all over some lemonade." Mel conciliated. "I hope there's plenty of chalk."

Three hours later, Mel was still explaining the proton batteries he had made for the ship, the induction magnets and how they worked with the repulsion engine that they were theoretically familiar with. Explaining complex aerospace engineering theory was amazingly simple to him and felt as good as stealing bases. Mel turned away from the chalkboard to the scientist's and despite the extensive diagrams he had drawn, they looked like they were completely lost.

"Why don't we get some lunch and come back to this."

The scientist's seemed eager for a break. "We could order in from Billy's" suggested Grover.

"How about Chinese?" Will Traggert added.

"Uh, had Chinese last night" Julia declared. "Let's go with Billy's."

By the time the server-bot got there with several packages of food, Mel did not feel like eating.

"Too much fun celebrating?" Asked Paul.

"Maybe. Anyway, I think I'll call it a day. You guys can wrestle over my equations until tomorrow."

Before Mel could open the exit door, he found himself in complete darkness. A female voice spoke to him. "Rest easy for a while. Your body needs to recuperate in order to continue."His consciousness was back in the modified Lillum tank. "How long have I been under?" He asked.

"Two days" came the answer.

"Wow, felt like it only a few hours, how's Silvia?"

"She's fine but ended her program six hours ago."

"Really? What's she doing?"

"She's in the recovery cycle"

Oh, well then, I won't continue. I'd like to join my wife."

"No problem Mister Raspalo, we just need to wait until your health signs are back to normal levels. We will induce you to sleep. It will enhance your recovery."

Four hours later, Mel and Silvia were making their way out of 'The Fountain of Unlimited Possibilities.'

"How do you feel?" He asked her.

"I feel great. Relaxed and rejuvenated."

"Yeah, me too."

Mel was eager to tell Silvia about his fulfilled dream of being a star baseball player in the World Series and a brilliant 'rocket scientist' as it were, but that he did not feel so smart now nor as athletic.

"What did you do?" He asked.

"Oh, just some research" she replied.

"What kind of research?"

Silvia blushed. "It was pioneering sexual research Mel. And I used my athletic young body to physically test my results."

"Ah" said Mel laughing, "No wonder you had to leave early."

Silvia joined in on the laughter. "I had such a great body Mel."

"You still do my love." They kissed.

"I'm glad you feel that way sweetie cause I've discovered some new things I'd like to try with you."

"Uh oh."

The two of them laughed some more and headed towards the robo-taxi waiting for them.

CHAPTER 45

Outside of the transport window, darkness prevailed but there was the constant stream of columns being passed with the accompanying noise of her vehicle speeding by them. Candra saw a field of tall grass outside and it reminded her of making love with Byryn in the Lillum tank after her battle with the reptilian woman. There were fire poles, a full moon, the smell of the fragrant grass, all adding to the intensity of their passion. She smiled remembering the smells and sensations.

"Arnie?"

Arnie came into view with no special effects. "Yes?"

"Did you erase the Byryn program?"

"Of course, you told me to. Having second thoughts?" A twin head popped up next to Arnie's head. One nodded and the other shook its head.

"No, never mind. I'll see what I can do with the human."

"You know he can't be programmed."

"We'll see about that."

The two heads looked at each other with surprise and then popped out of view.

CHAPTER 46

On the first serve, agent Bicks missed the ball by a wide margin. Fortunately, it was just outside of the service line and he would get another chance. He did not fare much better with the second serve. He managed to make contact with the ball, but it rolled on the ground towards the net and the game, set and match were over. Bicks walked towards the net and shook his opponent's hand saying what a good game it was. He could see that the man did not think it was a good game at all and he still disapproved of what Bicks was wearing. The players there were all in white tennis attire. Bicks wore cut-off blue jeans and a red t-shirt. That was fine with him. It was better than wearing the suit he normally donned. He wiped his brow thinking it might be a good time for a nice cold beer, preferably an ale but then noticed the redhead sitting on the sidelines wiping herself off with a towel. The beer could wait. She was tall, good looking, and wore a white halter and a short, white skirt.

'Hope she likes beer.' He thought.

He sat next to her but noticed his wrist-com trying to tell him something. He silenced it. She studied his clothing shaking her head. "Giving up already?"

Bicks grinned. "Yep, I figured I'd quit while I was ahead."

"You call losing badly being ahead?"

"Well, there's losing badly and there's being completely humiliated."

"Yeah, you weren't completely humiliated."

"No, not completely."

"You're not registered at this resort, are you?"

"Why" Bicks asked, "Was I that bad?"

She chuckled. "No, I haven't seen you here before, that's all."

"I spend most of my time in Kringle Kanyon."

"Where's that?"

"East side of Christmas World."

"Ah" she said disappointed, "you have kids."

"No, I work there. New programs oversight."

"Hmm, sounds nerdy."

"Oh yes, absolutely."

"You don't seem like the nerdy type. Why don't you tell me about some of your other interests over a drink."

"Beer?"

"Sounds perfect."

The robo-server in the sports bar close to the tennis courts had four arms, two to take orders with and two to serve. When it got to the table where Bicks was, it dropped off two tall ales and took away the two empty glasses while Bicks' newly acquainted friend was laughing.

"Anyone tell you that you have a peculiar sense of humor?"

Bicks took a sip of fresh beer before answering. "Only the ones who laugh."

"And the ones who don't?"

"Oh, they say I'm fucked up." She laughed again. "Damn good beer, " mentioned Bicks "but if you want a really good ale, you gotta go to Pub Alley."

"So I've heard."

"You've never been?"

She lifted her glass for a toast. "Not that I recall."

"So, Yolanda" Bicks asked, "What do you do when you're not playing tennis?"

"I travel."

"A traveling tennis player. How nice."

"My business takes care of itself."

"What kind of business is that, if I may ask?"

"I sell rare jewelry. My robo-reps handle all of the transactions."

"And I bet they're quite good at it."

"Actually, humans are better but, I don't have to put the bots up in hotels or feed them or pay for their vacations. On the other hand," she said leaning towards him, "I would hire a human like you."

Bicks leaned in as well. "I appreciate the offer but I'm a lousy salesperson."

"Oh, no doubt but I'm sure there are other things you're good at."

In a matter of minutes, they were in Yolanda's suite. She walked into the bedroom. "Put on some music, I'm going to change into something.... less. So what made you decide to come to this resort?"

Bicks talked to the music system while looking out at the view and down at the people in the pool. "Daylight by Lorenza Ponce." When he heard Lorenza's violin, he responded to Yolanda.

"I was just passing through and saw this amazing looking redhead."

"Quite the subtle, romantic type, are you?"

Bicks was trying to contact his PETA via his wrist-com but had no luck. "I guess."

Roberta came out in a see through negligee carrying a covered tray. "Thought you might like a little something." She brought the tray to Bicks and uncovered it. On the tray, cut up in pieces was his black PETA cat. "What's wrong agent Bicks, cat got your tongue?" She laughed and Bicks pulled out his gun. "Ahh come on, you know you can't harm me with that thing."

Bicks smiled. "Thought I'd give it a shot. Pun intended."

She put the tray down. "I guess you're not hungry but I am. Would you mind taking off your clothes? They give me indigestion."

Yolanda's eyes turned bright green and her body began to expand. Her four antennae grew out of her head and Bicks fired four shots at her. She responded by extending a tentacle towards him. "Come along, it'll all be over soon."

Bicks changed the setting on his gun. "Not if I can help it." The gun now fired a laser beam that scorched her tentacle and she withdrew it. The physimager grew to her full green slug-like form and started ripping up the floor to throw Bicks off balance. Bicks jumped through the large window in the living area and leapt over the railing while yelling "CLEAR THE POOL!" Guests who were using the pool saw glass splashing into the pool and Bicks falling towards it.

But before he could get halfway down, he was detained by a tentacle wrapped around his ankle. He fired a laser shot at his ankle and was released, but also screamed from the pain of the laser searing his flesh. Bicks splashed hard into the pool. He swam to the edge and climbed out limping. As he started to exit the pool area, he saw the physimager land in the pool making an enormous splash. The guests who were nearby, ran away terrified.

Out on the street Bicks yelled into his wrist-com. "EMERGENCY TRANSPORT, CODE SEVEN!" A nearby robo-taxi stopped and demanded the small family riding in it to exit the vehicle. It was the Feucks family on their way to Christmas World. Roland was not happy about the stalled vehicle. "WHAT! Are you kidding me? We're not going anywhere!"The robo-taxi was insistent. "I'm sorry sir. In a code seven emergency I cannot move this..."

After running with a limp to the taxi, Bicks opened the door and yelled at the family. "LOOK! RUN!!" The family saw the Physimager racing towards the vehicle on many legs it had grown.

When Lillie saw the giant green slug-like creature with a woman's head rapidly coming towards the taxi, she let out an ear-piercing scream. The family scrambled out of the taxi and ran down the street. Bicks got in. "I hope you know where I'm going." The taxi sped away just before the physimager could catch up with it. After he yelled 'Ozoz, on the double!' The robo-taxi sped along like it knew exactly where to go. Bicks rubbed his burned ankle wishing he had some kind of salve to ease the pain. Looking out of the glass ceiling and windows, he could not see the creature following. The

taxi eventually entered a rural area where there were few resi-
dences. The houses were two to three stories high with several
bedrooms and swimming pools. "If I get outta this alive, that's
where I'd like to stay. Maybe Ozoz will pay for it." Bicks muttered
hoping that somehow Ozoz would hear him. The houses became
sparser and finally there was a remarkably high metal wall they
drove to. An indistinguishable gate opened and there was a single
one story building with no windows at the end of a long driveway.
"Strange crib," he thought, "I hope O-Z has a nice cold beer waiting
for me."

Bicks stood before what was obviously a door. It was taller than
usual and there was no doorbell. The door opened but Bicks could
not enter. He felt a strong wind about him and felt talons sink into
his shoulders. Bicks screamed in agony as he heard the physimager's voice above him. "You didn't think you could get away from
me that easily did you?"

Bicks looked up and could see the creature, now resembling a siren.
She had the same face with the moving antennae but had a giant
eagle body. She began to lift Bicks but a laser tore through one of
her legs and she screamed while dropping Bicks. Candra slung her
laser rifle over her shoulder and pulled Bicks in while the physimager flew off.

"I see our guest has arrived."

"Yes," Bicks replied grimacing from the new pain in his shoulders.
"But don't put out the good linen."

It was a large room lightly decorated with white furniture and
white artwork. "Nice place you got here." Candra tore at Bicks shirt
until his wounds on his shoulders were fully exposed. She pulled
some salve out of her satchel and rubbed it over his wounds. "This
will make you feel better."

"A nice cold beer to go with it would....."

Before he could finish his words, the physimager burst through the front door. The oversized door of solid metal made an impact when it hit the floor. Before the physimager could grow tentacles to re-capture Bicks, Candra rushed him into another room and locked the door. Candra could hear him pounding on the door and screaming. "CANDRA, NO!!! NOOOOOO!!!"

Candra turned to her opponent. "Now it's just us girls."

The physimager barred her teeth. "Not for long."

Tentacles grew quickly out of the monster and she swung them at Candra. But Candra was adept at avoiding the blows. She ran, ducked, straightened up and fired her weapon. This went on for a brief while and the slug creature stopped. "I grow weary of this game." She picked up a couch and threw it at Candra who could not avoid the flying furniture and was slammed against the wall behind it. Candra pushed the couch away and tried to reach for her dropped weapon but was knocked against the wall again by a tenta-cle. The physimager coiled one of her tentacles tightly around Candra and lifted her off the floor until they were face to face. "Goodbye girlfriend."

The physimager plunged Candra into herself and Candra screamed. Bicks could be heard yelling in response to Candra's screams. The physimager pulled Candra out of herself and exam-ined Candra's plasmetal frame. "You're not even human!"

Candra smiled. "I have another surprise for you."

Candra exploded with such force, the door Bicks was behind in the adjacent room, flew off of its hinges but also protected him from the blast. Inside the detonated room, the paintings were burning on the wall, the furniture was in pieces, burning, and the physimager was in various sizes, small and large writhing around on the floor. The pieces of the creature, started moving towards each other and after sorting out which piece belonged where, she eventually and imperfectly, reformed herself. Her head crawled up top, re-attached itself and partially re-grew the long wild red hair with the four antennae moving about. The physimager made its way over to Bicks and removed the door off his unconscious form. She grew a tentacle and gently slapped him a few times.

"Wakey, wakey, I like my meat screaming."

Bicks desperately struggled to free himself from the tentacles tightly wrapped around him but started screaming as the physimager slowly sank him inside of herself. She smiled broadly.

"That's it."

Before she could consume the bottom part of his left leg, a star field opened up on one wall and a gravitational force began pulling everything out of the room into deep space. The smoldering paintings and furniture flew into the star field and the distinct voice of Ozoz could be heard ubiquitously. "Come San-gli, your time has arrived."

Bicks fell to the floor and held onto the door jamb as the door flew by him and into space. The Physimager grew a giant suction membrane across its bottom and was able to adhere herself to the floor and started to grow a tentacle to grab Bicks. However, the force of the gravitational pull yanked her away from Bicks and the room and she fell into the star field. The wall started to collapse and Bicks was beginning to get pulled into the star field. Startled by the sight of Candra's head rolling into the star field, Bicks lost his balance and the gravitational force pulled him towards the stars, but a wall formed before he entered the event horizon. Bicks slid down the wall onto the floor and passed out.

CHAPTER 47

The three-dimensional screen in Phillimus Mekkel's office was active again. He was occupying the center space and the image of his cat-like face was larger than the representative shareholders on the screen. "Representatives, you have already received the stat-graphs indicating the current tourist index on Maze. As you can see over the last few weeks, despite the fear of losing revenue, there has been an increase in visitors and henceforth an increase in revenue. There are many rumors floating about as to why this has occurred. One of the more popular being, a new game featuring a monster on the loose gobbling up some of our visitors."Mekkel waited for a few chuckles to subside. "While there have been a few documented reports of disappearances, a full investigation of the matter has proven to be inconclusive. However, due to our re-doubled efforts to form Maze into a more secure and accountable amusement planet, we presently have reason to believe that these mysterious disappearances have ceased."

"Also, according to an independent research firm analysis included in your report, there is no reason to believe that the current tourist index will drop off anytime soon in the foreseeable future. With this in mind, I hereby propose a moratorium on the proposed dissolution of the Maze limited general partnership. I will give you time to look over the numbers before casting your vote." On the screen, an active discussion followed the chairman's speech. Mekkel's face became the size of the other members. Kelde walked into his office and Mekkel adjusted his com so the members could not hear their conversation. "Have you contacted the victim's families?" Kelde poured himself a drink. "Yes, they have all accepted our version of the unfortunate circumstances as well as the monetary compensation, that is, with the exception of the Dubois family. They don't want nor need the money. They want a permanent memorial set up here on Maze."Mekkel frowned. "What kind of memorial?" Kelde sat and looked pleased with himself. "I suggested a new and permanent amusement adventure dedicated to the young couple with a plaque and statue of them at the entrance." Mekkel turned back to the screen voicing sarcasm. "Can't wait to hear about this. Hold on, votes are coming in."

Below the images of all twenty-two MazeCor reps, the word 'affirmative' could be seen. As usual, there were three members absent and their images were blank. In essence, the partners had agreed to a moratorium on the proposed dissolution of the Maze partnership and Mekkel's face returned to its larger size on the screen before he spoke. "It is agreed then. MazeCor will continue as a limited partnership under the rules and guidelines as set forth in our by-laws. This agreement will be in effect until the next scheduled general partnership session. This conference is hereby adjourned until said time."

There was petty conversation but the members on the screen blacked out almost all at once. The silence was a relief to Mekkel who could now only hear the ice clinking in Kelde's drink. Kelde's spoke quietly and his speech was slightly affected by his drink. "Despite your reservations, I think you've managed to hang on to your job, boss."

"Yes, and this proposed memorial?"Kelde stood up walked the few steps in Mekkel's direction and placed an ad-tab on his desk. Mekkel looked at it and saw fictionalized images of the plaque memorializing Sheela and Shakree Dubois and their bronze statues directly behind it. A dozen feet away stood another figure constructed to resemble and move in a restricted manner like the physimager. Above it read a sign;

THE PHYSIMAGER IN LIVE ANIMATRONICS. TERROR AND ADVENTURE LIKE YOU'VE NEVER EXPERIENCED BEFORE.

Mekkel could not help but smile as he turned to Kelde. "The rumors about this might catch up with the reality my friend."Kelde finished off his first drink. "By then, we will have retired with so much money, it will hardly matter will it?"

The screen lit up both of their faces and their hopes as if they had been bathed in the neoteric light of revivified existence.

CHAPTER 48

Mozilli stood up at police headquarters. He looked at the badge and gun on his desk with a knowing smile and reached out to shake Felker's hand. "You're sure I can't talk you into an extended leave with pay?" Felker looked down at the ambi-cast on his leg and could still feel the hurt of his repaired ribs but he spoke with reluctance. "Yes sir, I'm sure. I'll be by to visit after a while but I'm looking at semi-retirement. It's been a..." Felker almost teared up. "Well, let's just say it's been one hell of a ride sir."

"Yeah, that it has been. Take care of yourself Felk."

Felker smiled and walked with a barely noticeable limp out of Mozilli's office just as Mozilli sat trying to figure out what flavor of Tylenol lollipop he should try. When Felker got to the exit, Wex was waiting for him. Like Felker, he had some obvious lumps and scars but appeared to be in better shape. "So, figured out where you're going hotshot?" Wex looked more animated than usual. The time off work must have done him some good. Felker carefully negotiated coming down the steps. "What are you doing here?"

"Came to see you off, like an old ugly girlfriend. It was fun but glad to see you go."

Felker laughed. "You'll miss me."

"For sure. You haven't seen the young dick they've assigned me with."

"My hearts bleeding can you tell?"

"Felk, you have to have a heart for it to bleed."

"Ouch. See you around Wex. Take care of yourself."

"Yeah, I'll do that.

Felker got into an auto-cab and waved to Wex who just smiled. He adjusted his wrist-com and started his favorite soap. "Spaceport" he blurted out to the bot-driver.

CHAPTER 49

Special agent Brian Bicks had a real human push him along in his wheelchair at the spaceport. Her name was Clarissa and she was young, pretty, exceptionally courteous and every time he would look up at her, he thought he should figure out a way to stay on the pleasure planet. After Captain Mozilli told him that this attendant was free for the next two weeks, she smiled genuinely at the suggestion. But every time Bicks would look up at her pretty young face, he was reminded of the only real woman he had been with in his life as a GBI agent, Candra. That loss caused him to insincerely smile back at Clarissa who undoubtedly thought he was still feeling the pain of losing the lower part of his left leg. He did feel strangeness and numbness in his leg but the pain was deeper than that. And, he still had clouded nightmares about what had happened to Candra. He told Mozilli that there was a terrible explosion and he was captured by the physimager. After that, all he remembered was waking up in a hospital.

They told him that it was a miracle that he was still alive. He believed that, but also believed that Ozoz had something to do with saving him as well as ridding Maze of the physimager. The creature had mysteriously disappeared. Bicks also felt that Maze was not the place for a handicapped man. Of course, the lower part of his left leg had been replaced with plas-metal and he was informed that this new lower appendage would work better than the original but that would take some time getting used to. Time and rehabilitation. And even though the chairman himself had convinced the GBI heads that he would receive full medical benefits and recovery time on Maze, Bicks decided to return to the GBI and wait for his next assignment.

Clarissa had rolled him closer to the check-in point. He saw the woman who banged into him when he first arrived. She looked at him with sympathetic smile and Bicks assumed that she thought he should have stayed with her on this trip. Maybe she was right. He also saw the Feucks. The young girl, Lillie, seemed to be content with her oversized doll that was talking to her but the parents looked to be unsettled, preoccupied. At least they would not have to work ever again in their lives. MazeCor had seen to that. Bicks was sure that they had to sign the same non-disclosure documents that he had to. The physimager would remain a well-kept secret that would stay on Maze. Not even the GBI would know about it. Except Bicks, he would know and remember that creature forever and of course, the woman he lost to it. There were other people getting in line to board the shuttle to take them away from Maze. Some he recognized, most he did not. There was an older couple and a young man who had arrived with a companion who was now alone. He did not look too pleased.

'Welcome to the club' thought Bicks. Clarissa was getting security clearance to take Bicks up the ramp where he would board the shuttle. She would smile, regretfully say goodbye to him and perhaps even give him a soft kiss before walking away. Real women. Bicks would go back to his programmed companion in his Lillum tank. She would help him rehabilitate. Help him to even see love again but somehow the idea left a bad taste in his mouth that he could not swallow.

CHAPTER 50

Approximately sixteen miles above Maze, the O.R.E.S. 1600 was using its mandibles to sort through space debris. Through the use of its magnoscanner, it ignored the living room furnishings passing by but did pay attention to a creature floating by. Inside of the ship, the physimager could be seen on various screens. Arnie, singing Nessun Dorma from Turandot and dressed for the occasion, scanned for any signs of life in the creature. He observed its mis-shaped, pale face and vacant eyes but not finding any life signs, he returned to the business of putting Candra back together. She was on a large operating table with several thin, robotic arms inserting plas-metal body parts. By the time he had finished the song, Candra was complete. Arnie took the appropriate bows to thunderous applause for the singing and the successful operation.

"And now, how do I turn this girl on? Oh yeah! Wake up bee-yach!"

Candra sat up slowly. "What did you just call me?"

"Nothing, oh, *be-yond*. As in beyond beautiful. I think I've out done myself this time. I think I deserve a raise."

"Only raise you're gonna get is from my middle finger."

"Oh! Such ingratitude! You think it was easy finding your blowed up ass out here in the middle of nowhere?" You gotta a lotta nerve honey girl! See if I even *think* about reassembling your poor blowed up butt again. The nerve of some people! Don't even get a...."

"Thank you, Arnie."

"Say what?"

"I said thank you." Candra looked through her small closet of chainmail dresses and picked one that had a blue tint to it. "Don't act like you deaf. You record everything I say."

"That's right." He re-played Candra's voice. 'Thank you, Arnie.' "Yes, I'm going to play it every time you forget to say it which is way too often." 'Thank you, Arnie,' "Sounds good don't it?"

'Thank you, Arnie.'

Candra was at the com. "Sounds annoying. Yowwee Zowwee, looks like Ozoz has paid up and included a bonus. Let's go planet side and spend some of this money. Oh, and pay off that scumbag who sent me the Pi-One transmission. Send it in the slowest way possible."

"I'll do it after I replay those magic words."

"What?"

Arnie replayed Candra's voice. 'Thank you, Arnie."

"You said you wanted a raise?"

"I think I deserve one."

"What are those magic words again?"

Arnie started singing "Thank you" (Falettinme Be Mice Elf Agin) by Sly and the Family Stone. His image could be seen throughout the ship's screens. He was wearing bright-blue, low-cut bell bottom jeans, a tie-dyed long sleeve shirt with wide lapels with glitter all over the front and back. He had on tall black boots and a red silk scarf on his head. There was a band behind him wearing similar clothing. Candra put on a huge Afro, some beads and adjusted her dress so that it undulated rainbow colors. She got up and started dancing as the ship retracted its mandibles and headed in a descent towards Maze.

After several hours and not having to show 'papers,' Candra entered the spaceport still wearing her afro and still humming Sly and the Family Stone who was being covered by Arnie on her wrist-com. She had a bounce in her step and the long beads she was wearing, responded to her movement. Everything about her seemed to sparkle with excitement. But before she got on the escalator to join the mad mush of masses on the ground, that sparkle was replaced with heat, the kind that comes from feeling that you don't belong, from humiliation and from wanting something you can't have. Because directly in her line of sight was the man she thought she was in love with, Brian Bicks, kissing a young beautiful woman from the wheelchair he was sitting in. She turned away, not being able to watch and slowly took off her wig. Her chainmail dress became a dull chrome. She could still hear all of the people around but everything seemed to become quiet as she slumped down until her chest was touching her knees. Her mouth could taste fresh tears enter her lips and Arnie's music faded away.

"Candra" Arnie quietly spoke to her. "Candra."

Candra had trouble getting the words out. "What do you want?"

"You need to talk to him."

"What are you talking about?"

"Come on honey girl, you didn't come all the way down here just to spend some money. You and I both know you came down here to see Brian Bicks. And, if you don't go over there and talk to him, you will never see him again. Ever."

"He's busy."

"Turn around."

"He doesn't even know what I am!"

"Candra, you are way better than anything he's ever had in his entire life. TURN AROUND!"

Candra wiped her face, stood up and turned to see Brian Bicks staring at her. She paused for a moment and then ran to him. Before attempting to give him a hug from his seat, he insisted on standing.

He did so and they kissed slowly and passionately as if they had been deprived of breathing. When Brian pulled slightly away from her, he could see the tears streaming down her face.

"I thought you were....."

"Don't say it." Candra whispered in his ear.

He paused and looked back. "I think I might have missed my flight."

"No, you haven't. You've been.... reassigned."

Bicks smiled. "Yeah, are there um... perks on this reassigned flight?"

Candra started walking him back towards her ship's gate. "You betcha, for starters, I've reinstalled the Byryn program. It's now called the Brian program."

"That's a good start."

"That, is just the beginning."

Arnie remotely contacted Brian's wheelchair and sent it to where it came from. He dressed himself in bishop's attire and started humming "Here Comes the Bride"....

Candra gave him a sharp look. "Arnie!"

www.ingramcontent.com/pod-product-compliance
Lightning Source LLC
Chambersburg PA
CBHW020909160726
47993CB00005B/1890